Pearls of an unstrung necklace

Pearls of an unstrung necklace

by

Prakash Kona

fugue state press
new york

ISBN 1-879193-14-0

Library of Congress Control Number 2004113107

Front cover photograph: "River Tay Pearls,"
Copyright © 1996 by Dr. W.H. Findlay; from *The Heritage of Perth*, published by Perth & Kinross District Libraries.
Used by permission.

Back cover painting: anonymous Madhubani artist

Fugue State Press
PO Box 80, Cooper Station
New York NY 10276

Website: www.fuguestatepress.com
Email: info@fuguestatepress.com

Printed in the United States of America

Pearls of an unstrung necklace

The Tiger and the Cave

Who was the tiger and what was the cave? The black-striped tiger from where the sun rises and the cave of blue seas. In the rising sun the stripes turn orange and brown. The cave is a diamond of asymmetrical shape with dark glitter in bright light. The tiger smelt the mouth of the cave from a distance. The mouth of the cave knew that the tiger was on its way. In the dark the cave was resplendently dark paling the darkness outside. The eye of the tiger was smooth as a glider in the concavity of valleys. The tiger and the cave communicated in their cosmic differentiality. In the depths of its imagination the cave felt a need for the tiger. Was it a need or a precondition of being? Was the need for the cave built into being of the tiger? Beings need beings. The cave preconceived the tiger. In the veins of the tiger the cave was there latent in its potency as the colored stripes of the tiger. The tiger was lost in the cave. The cave was never waiting for the tiger. They were reluctant to complement one another in time or space because that meant being reduced to oneness outside the realms of dark. The laws of dark superseded the idea of need and condition of being. They were screens that the dark chewed into cud whenever it was hungry. Being is structured within need. That's what makes it to be. The mouth of the cave looked into eyes of the tiger. The eyes bowed with shyness that deep love produces in the faces of lovers. It was a sense of being overwhelmed by something that was far from itself. The femininity of the tiger was in its claws. The cave was thick-lipped and sang melodies of days of dark dainties and nights of nimble natties. The tiger scratched its way into the cave. The cave was amused with the tiger's impetuosity. With its nature the tiger endeared itself to the cave. For the tiger the cave was reality of a symbol. The tiger was far from the cave. Distance stood in inverse relationship to being. The further the tiger went the closer the cave to its being. The marks of the tiger's body were imprinted on the rock of the cave. I am the tiger in the heart of the cave. You are the cave in the soul of the tiger.

The Palmist

On the pavement outside the gates of a park the palmist sat
in the shade of a tree with a parrot in a cage that picked up
the fortune of a person from a pack of cards. The educated
view is that palmists are face-readers. They read the face of
the client and provide language for expressions of that face
taken from a discourse. My face is my fortune. I can
dissemble and change the outcome of my fortune. An
alternate view is that the palmist reflects the discourse of
human sciences because she functions based on the theory
of probability. The truth may be that somewhere between
face reading and probability the palmist arrives at the state
of luck in my life. In the end what has luck to do with my
palm? Where does my palm come into picture? What do
the lines say outside the discourse of lines? Is there a line
that looks like the shape of my friend's name? One line that
will capture something of my friend is enough to captivate
my heart. The lips or fingers or outlook of my friend.
Something other than a photographic reproduction of a
certain mood in my friend. I know those moods. Every one
of them is stored in memory. Those moods run to hundreds
of lines and thousands of pages. I recall them the instant I
see the friend. I want the palmist to look into my eyes and
tell me the fortunes of my friend. My friend lives in my
eyes. The palmist is beguiled by the idea of mother that I
project in relation to my friend. I am childless. How can I
impose childhood upon my friend? How can that one stop
being my child? I tell my friend: you are *it*. *It* is not a child.
It is a woman or a man. *It* can do without me. I cannot live
without *it*. *It* is you my friend that my words dare not
appropriate. *It* is smoke from a forest fire somewhere in the
mountains. *It* is spring showing her skirts to eyes that have

just woken up. *It* is you love more than my love. *It* you are a fish in waters of my soul. The fortunes of my palm stand bare without you in them. I give you my love as gift to myself. That's what it means to love you.

Colors for Sounds

The color of echo is the bat in the recesses of dark coming
out as black. Black echoes to white music. Color carries the
weight of sound. The sound of color is in magnitude a lamp
floating on a river at night. The festival of lights begins at
night. Night echoes with sounds of crackers. The bats are in
hiding. In a night of light the bat is not at home in dark.
Betrayed by the dark for a night the bat goes back to the
blackness it comes from. On a night blacker than your eyes
closed I fell in love with a dream.
Red is the fruit of pining. I pined for you in the youthful
ignorance that you were a light that the moth had to
approach with caution. I opened a red door. The sweet
weight of your passion gave my blood-red eyes a reason to
stay awake. I could murder for a shot of sleep. I preferred to
die for a kiss. In the sunset on a bridge above a railway
track blood circulated from your body into mine. I was in
your heart never to leave.
The poison of separation turned the body to blue. The
shifting shades of blue sky were an antidote to pain of
separation from you. I was orange and you were green.
Your greenness on my orange turned to a leaf on a rose
plant. Your thoughts have turned blue this afternoon. If I
made you sad I apologize with all my body. My body was
wretched at the thought of separation. Forgive my body and
accept the blue roses of her love for you. The sky cast a
blue spell on you and me. Shades of shifting memories take
us to the blue moon. The night is blue. The song from the
house nearby refreshed my love for you. I slept with you in
blue dreams on blue rafts with blooming lights
of a coastline in view.
Violet is the color of time. The wild times that we were

together with white sunlight changing to purplish blue and
mauve. You were violet of the forest. I smelt
you in the sweat of my skin.
I saw the world with yellow eyes. I burnt with prejudice
against a world that did not accept me for who I am. My
eyes turned yellow. I was jaundiced. I hated nothing like I
hated gold. It symbolized the world for me. I was glad that
the philosopher's stone was never found. It would have
been a shame to turn my love into gold or silver. My love is
the sun. I am moon that takes its reflection from the light of
sun. My love the sun has touched my soul with freshness of
washed linen. The tinge of yellow in the moon is the sun
harboring itself within me. I give up the world for
the sun that is my world.
My graying hair reminds me of death to come. Quiet
passions are gray. Death is colorless as water. Colorless
sounds are ghosts in a silent room. My hair tells me that I'm
ready to say goodbye. I persist in the strange absence of
things that characterizes my life. Gray waters remind me of
black hair of love. I loved and never lost. Deathless is my
love. While I die my love remains proof that
I once was a queen.

Moments

Moments are made of miracles. A shadow on a curtain talks to you at night. At the heart of silence is a word for silence to know it is silence. Silent silences are miracles performed through sounds. Why must silence know itself? Unknowingly I drift from miracle to miracle. Silence responds to silence. Dreams write letters to dreams about dreams. I am a black wave roughing the rocks of a cave shaping them as the night does to thorns in the briar giving them a look of vulnerability. My happy moments are passing shadows and sad moments are stones at the bottom of a pool. My writing suffers when you move from passivity to activity.

A hot angel descends from the mountain to abide in the kitchen. There are no beds in the kitchen but we made love to the smell of food in the background. In the rub of bodies the food was cooked. We did not eat. We took in the aroma of bodies on fire. It was a moment above all moments. In vulnerable caves we swooned in paroxysms of madness. The caves led to seas. Was the sea my self or was I contriving an escape to new lands where you resided as travelers normally do? Did the traveler return home towards end of night? Was her home where she thought it was? Homes were lost when the body of earth quaked. Was the earth alone or did a passing star that gazed lovingly move her body? Your fingers on my neck sliding to my breast. The traffic in background with the day moving by. In the room it is night. You and me in one breast in one garden in one single moment. One is the way that one looks at one. There is no one in reality. You are not one drop of rain. You are poetry of water running along streets without a sense of direction. I am the street that receives the water as blessing from clouds. Will the cloud envy the happiness of my burning breast? We screamed but the night did not return the scream. Echoes were hiding in wind. The wind swept the faces of hills with moisture from seas. We were something other than ourselves. We were bread in the mouths of children. The music that rouses the cobra to dance was within us. The cobra of passion was ready to strike at the halting of music. In distinct silence we heard what soul said to body. The night reproduced the stillness of our lives. The lava solidified into rock with the night cooling the craters of passion. Does night let the lovers wake? I sleep to voices of children ready to go to school. I wake to sight of birds returning home. My beloved is anxious. Problems of living plague the soul of beloved. The beloved complains of dangerous times. What pregnant thoughts occupy the soul of the beloved? The imagination is poor because my beloved does not respond to words. Hungry is the beloved for a moment of forgetfulness. My words are incapable of that moment. I call you to complain that I never hear from you. You hear to tell me that my words do not mean what they say. Our moments do not correspond to one another. In you I love that which does not complement. I put words in your mouth. I smell the saliva of your mouth in them. In your mouth my words have changed. They have the taste of raw guavas. In the dawn the day communicates with night. Transitory shadows are born in that moment. That which intersects with another cancels itself out at a certain point. What happens to another? The beloved lives among people who work for a living. I am a parasite that thrives on words. Useless are my moments. My sense of personal worth comes from watching you come to terms with your realities. Momentarily I disappear. You are there with a puzzled expression attached to a smile. Our arms know each other only too well. They embrace without being told. In pink sunlight shadows depart never to return for the moment has passed. There is a slight chill in the air that comes through the open door.

Eroticized in a cistern of purple light. The island of birds and the stranger to words. The body that is mine. I take you into a sacred tunnel. The eyes felt more naked than the body they looked at. The body is shocked by nakedness of eyes. Between the eyes in what does not see and cannot be seen is my love. The world avoids your stare but I search for your glance. I am nothing. In loving you I become something. Lost in labyrinths of tomorrow which is yesterday posing as today I wish for the tenderness of a moment in sea. I take from you freedom of love that comes from my aloneness. I am redundant as smoke when you are away. Does love need to be embodied in reality for it to be love? The technology of love is restricted to senses. Once your body transformed into wilderness through you I created possibilities of survival. The wilderness was not to be touched without strange defiance. That is another language. It comes from the way things are. Discontinuity is what I suffer from. In pieces I wrote about peace. Warring within myself I reconstructed miniature islands of peace. What happened to birds that were there before consciousness corrupted my childhood? I don't understand how I entered your equation. I don't want to be personalized by God or man or woman. Do I really exist outside you? Is there a person that is me who is in fact nothing? I become something in your love. I ask the rose of friendship from one I love. The one I love rocks the cradle that has no baby in it. Eccentricities are lovable when they stand out as imperfections on lovely faces. I love your eccentricities. I could sit and make stories of all kinds just watching them until sleep the enemy of lovers must consume me. The baby that does not exist walks out of cradle. Does it become man or woman or a mixture of both is an open question. Were you a child before you became the one you are? I saw the child. I did not see you. I can love a child. How can I be in love with a child? What if I confessed to you that I was child as well. Would it make a difference to the way you receive me in your arms? You might feel left out or misunderstood. I cannot calculate the moments of your body because that would be devastatingly unreal for someone as virtual as I am. I am the spit image of words I use. You are the missing component of words that compose me. You must be the child I was. Your arms will not accept me as woman. How can I be the child you are and still be myself. I must go beyond the culture of my body to know who you are. Out of the range of conflict I see your body with love of a mother. With passing of the mother I become a woman. Traces of mother you feel in my tender touches. Does mother make love to child in terms that are less than metaphorical? I woke up in heaven only to forget the fact I was in a state of sleep. With the disappearance of heaven I slept as if I was never awake to begin with. Your body is sleep that is always sleep with no knowledge of ever awakening. Your body is that waking that has never slept at all. They are absolute states not complementary ones. We kiss until the innermost resources of our souls are spent. The parting is implicit in your moving away to the other side of bed.

Salt, Sunlight, Pendulum

I cannot be your mirror image because it is illusion. In the prison of time thoughts of salt bring tears to eyes. Salt is principle of realism. Though I have a musical sense of moodiness death offers certainty for life to go on. In glimpses of reality I found happiness of dreams. I taste salt of eyes when sunlight invades the privacy of home disrespecting the norm that guest must not enslave host.

You are sunlight that occupies space without being occupied. In my home I am your hostage. How could I be without knowing that you cherish anger as ghost would cherish the body it left behind? How could you be without possessing me? We are caught in nature of things. The pendulum is without nature. It swings with unimprovised movements of a sleepwalking dancer. In case of pendulum the idea is also object. The pendulum transcends distinction between ideal and real. It stands out as exception among objects. Unsteady at heart I envy the pendulum. Wars and famines will not disturb its timeless constancy. I am hurt that I don't see you enough. I want to be suspended in a way as to regulate the beating of time's heart. Time is heartless. My sweet moments with you pass away as if they never existed. My nature drops dead into the state of a pendulum which seriously means I must be aging. I am saved by saltiness of salt made in hot rays of sunlight. It means that I love you despite the fact that I am invaded and occupied. We have seen too much of each other. At the end of lovemaking sessions my hands need to sleep and you wish to talk and be entertained. There is a crack in our expectations. The same body I see every day and convince myself that it must be a different one. The approach to loving a person is stressful enough. I need to rest and I don't want you to mistake it for indifference. I can live with a friend and not a lover. Befriend me as salt befriends sunlight. You don't have to invade or occupy for me to love you. You had it before I set my eyes on you. Space is not an issue for me. My sense of privacy is internal to my nature. Deprived of nature I turn into a pendulum. Forgive my unfairness if I speak for you. I manipulate when you don't look. I entice you toward me. I decide that I need you and convey the same to you. You are moved. Have I invaded and occupied you? In that hoarse voice of lovemakers you say yes. Love that is not love is a pendulum. The words we use are in a crisis. We talk of change without thinking of sea. I am waters of the sea. For you I become salt. The sad motion of pendulum tells me that something has been changing all along. I was mistaken. My theories of nature are wrong. I confess that I am deceived by eyes of imagination. To know you as verity I must renounce deception. Water is nature of salt. Salt is nature of sunlight. The pendulum connects all. In love I am not a prisoner of time. This has nothing to do with words. I am water at deepest level of who I am. From the underground water moves into public taps for life to continue. That is my humanity. Loving you is not about being human. It is about loving you. It is knowledge that you precede me. The water does not precede salt and sunlight. The soundless motion of pendulum precedes the coming of day or salt that I eat with bread, hot chilies and water. You are time and I am your prisoner.

Analysis of Sleep

I am divided as scales of a fish. Walls collide in moonless madness. I am divided as moons of planets that fish their way in cosmic waters. Using the scales of a fish I proved for a fact that mathematically speaking bodies cannot be multiplied with souls. The soul is knowledge of body. The body experiences the perceiving eye in moments. There is no water in paradise. The dancers are reluctant to please the gods. Flushed cheeks on indifferent nights. Insomnia bothers me. I find you distraught and far away. You are earth and I am moon. The onslaught of sensuality on my weeping nerves. The soul is a pathetic onlooker. Suffering bodies sing strange songs. I am divided within my own self. Where do you come from that you produce such disturbance within me? You sent ripples through sleeping waters of cosmos. Where do you hide your face when I need to see you most? What happens to my whirling feet when I seek to find you everywhere? I never stop. Neither do the feet. We share the fate of travelers. I can find you in different faces at different points in life. My search begins each time we meet. When you are away I am thinking that only death can stop my feet. I apologize to you if I die before knowing you. The impassioned face of age speaks to me in a disconnected tone. Am I really in the present where I am supposed to be? The heart creates its own ways in and out of reality. Speak to me and let me be real for moments that I am with you. The body is in terror when it realizes that soul has been watching it all along. I look for reasons to complain to you especially after long absences. I forget my complaints the instant I see you. You point out the fact that the lover in me changes with time. You mean to say that the intensity of the lover's body diminishes before noonday sun. I am no match for the sun. I suggest that it is high time you choose the sun for lover rather than me. The unflagging energy of sun will pronounce words of unending love that might remotely satisfy your soul. In cosmic time the sun is limited. In the universe how do you define a limitation if one form is always changing to another. I cannot stop myself from touching water. The water has life of its own. It speaks to me as if words mattered. It demands love of me. I ought to express myself as clearly as possible. The demands of water are infinite. I can choose to be water that passes. A coldness that is incompatible with spirit torments my body. I am not sure if I want to be touched by the sky. How can I be water without longing for blueness of sky. I am disappointed by contradictions that soul has set for body. Pushed to the brink of a state without words my body blurts out a confession of true love for you. Dim lights are melancholic at dawn. My body looks forward to nothing. The cream of days is over. It is nothing or you. I look at you. My seriousness has a subtle effect on your palate. You are hungry for no reason at all. Lovers have no weather to claim for themselves. Love weathers all. The poetry of death is voice of the person missed in waterless paradise without a dancer. I live to stand by your side and watch the sun go to sleep in mountains among bushes and stones before waking up to light the lamp of day.

Reciprocities

Empires are in love with dust. Empire-builders are sentimental men affected by the way things are. The backdrop of failure makes the fall of empire as real as folly of the empire-builder. No one contributes to the lifeblood of future but one who cannot distinguish dust from a dream. She functions in awareness that dust can be as deathless as dreams. The fate of lovers is determined by the timing of day. The day blurs into night with closing eyes of a watchman. The night bursts upon day with a bouquet of flowers. I give a thing that you may forget the thing. You remember the thing and you forgive me for expecting to be remembered. The thing is broken with time. The memory of the thing is intact. I rejected the thing before I gave it to you. You took it as gift that I very well knew you deserved. I received your time. In the brief span that you were with me I forgot all things. I could not forget you. I forgot myself. It was as if I had never been there. Only later the fact of memory appeared on scene. At those memorable points that I spent with you there was no memory. The things we do for memory. The sacrifices that memory demands of us are bewildering. I sacrifice memory for the joy of being with you. In the end empire-builders meet the same fate as lovers. Their dreams are dust. Out of dust of dreams I will rebuild the empire of love. I will derail the wheels of fate with a grain of sand. Why is that you never want things I give you? The absent gaze makes me feel that I offer a gift that is all but myself. I locked my heart with a picture of you within me and the keys are with you. Isn't that more than myself. You smile to assuage my conflicts. The smile hurt more than salt on wounds. I give you my wounds as tokens of memory. My pain is of little use to you. On the brighter side you need my pain to know your beautiful self. My pain is only a word. It is long gone. This might be romantic justification for irresponsibility in an all too real world. The warm days of winter and the cool days of summer constitute a version of love. I cannot give myself to you. I can give you to yourself. I can reciprocate a gesture that I do not see. The presence of the gesture is real as a rain cloud. In the gift of a gesture I changed the direction of my life. The elements of life would not leave me alone. In earth I became soil. In water I was liquid. In air I was breeze. In sky I was color. In fire I was heat. The elements that were me precipitated into music that was sweet murder of this useless body of mine. I did not die for you. I died for a thought. A thought in me died for you. In those billions of times that your eyes move around there is one look that I don't understand. I dare not give that look words. I cannot stop from searching into that look for meaning that can sustain music that murders me. The certainty of death I offer you. I could also give you my failure to understand you as a gift of all gifts. I choose to die for knowledge that had nothing to do with words. It was knowledge where colors existed for sounds. The fluidity of circumstances with a secret order governs the cult of your being. I belong to that cult at crossroads smoking marijuana and watching nightmares with disdain.

A camera for inner states of the soul. The pastures where gods roam at nights. I wrote letters in dark. Words that could not be seen became a source of life for the lantern. Did life begin in an aperture in a rock from where you could see pink faces of mountains at dawn? Roads roll by as if they were days of old. On a rolling road I stood and waited for a bus to reach the edge of civilization. The light was gray and I crossed a playground before I reached one house on the other side of civilization. In extraordinary uncertainty where the only order was that of a cave in a rock from where civilization could be seen at a distance we spoke in mindless syllables. I love you as person but not the person that your name stands for. The dusk without name is dusk at the end of day. Those particular moments of our lives are lost in wilderness of ages. Names are forgotten. You are nameless dusk on the other side of civilization in a cave within a rock. The civilized world of names means nothing to you. In your namelessness I became one with you. That was the beginning of a storm that threatened to rout out civilization itself. In the civilized world the noise that names produce rumbled against one another. Pleasure is a vague idea in the context of painful social realities. The storm threatened to rout out all existing notions of pleasure. The storm retained itself. We wandered through worlds without words. Time was a joke. We joked about beginnings and endings. The joke did not have syntax. The joke had a convoluted logic that was meant to be convoluted. The joke of my love met eye-to-eye with the joke of my life. We laughed the laughter of the truly uncivilized. In the eyes of universe everything is just a state of mind except jokes that we make to kill time. Was infinite pain of my grieving heart just a state of mind. I ask this question as if it were a rhetorical one. I am a drunkard thriving on magic of symbols. Beautiful are mistakes of the beautiful. Civilization was a mirage for a lover who saw the world through an aperture in a rock. That which is real when seen through the eye of a rock can only be the face of a lonely and wandering god. Civilization smarts with pain in the divine gaze. As a person of God I did not care to be civilized. I walked to the house on the other side of civilization where you lived. I am hard as the heart of a man. You the divine. I love you. The hardness of man in me is broken in the dark. I betrayed God. You my lover I succumb to you. My heart is a rock with an aperture for you to enter. Inside this rock is a gentle stream. There are no fish in this stream. These waters are meant for lips of lovers. They are meant to cool fires of the lover's tongue. I was a fish that belonged to the ocean. I outlived the stream when through the aperture in the rock I found my way to the ocean. In my blood there remained waters of the stream.

I am the rock of love. I bear the pain of life without illusions when I am with you. Time wears me. I stand the pain of slow destruction. I am a monster that gorges food when I am exhausted at the thought of finding the kind of love that suits my heart. I am two-dimensional. I am rock on outside and stream inside. My hands are hard when they touch you. I approach you as a perennial stream of petals brushing the skin of your body. My soul is a vase of petals. I throw them at your feet. I kiss the petals that your feet have touched. In the stream of floating petals I feel a pair of dark eyes looking at me. Moved by the look I turn into a dewdrop falling from your eyes. On earth I solidify into a rock with an aperture made hollow by eyes that have wept for you.

The Bank

The eyes have eaten before tongue tasted. Eyes that are
faces within faces. The hunger of eyes is insatiable. The
tongue suffers in the process of complementing eyes. Food
and love are economic questions. They are bound to
institutions guided by norms. The eyes feed upon what
belongs to the tongue. The territory of tongue is lost to eye.
The tongue looks at the world that eyes have consumed.
The passion of tongue is enflamed when it watches eyes
ingest the world. The food of eyes and love of the tongue.
The possessive eye and tongue on fire. Empty bellies
cannot make love. This is the assumption fundamental to
philosophy as study of the production of the word in
political economy. The 'I' flourishes in succulence of the
tongue. The tongue reaps fruits of eyes. The limpid waters
of eyes salt the sweet loves of tongue. I taste you with eyes.
I love you with the tongue. When you left the world was a
blank screen. The last ray of light disappeared from surface
of earth. The audience left while my eyes were glued to
screen. My eyes refused to let go of nothing. I was clinging
to a raft while currents threw me in every possible
direction. I was tongue-tied when my eyes saw those
moments we spent together in dark rooms with dim light
from streets. Clothes are redundant to naked body. In dark
the tongue lashes eyes of the other. With my tongue I see
you. With your eyes you receive me. My eye burns for
wetness of your tongue. Your tongue is tickled by fluttering
of my eyes. In each word I write I give you fire of my
tongue. In each written word I see a soft stare coming out
as gentle light. Do we blend into a new form like color of
tealeaves in boiling water? My tongue cherishes bitterness
of milkless tea each morning. My eyes ruminate the

objective world as it disappears into openings of my body. Out gushes forth a world of objects banked by eyes. In the river of tongue objects sink without exception. The bosom of the river swells when shadow of the cloud passes over it. The eye accepts the gift of the spectacle of tongue swelling in passion. The tongue returns the gift of eye with sounds far from any distinct meaning. The tongue along with its counterpart the eye made a pact to destroy the bank in the neighborhood. It was customary for bankers to observe profiles of customers and speak about issues related to security of property-related values in a society that was getting more and more dangerous by the day. The tongue spat with anger and eye wept with anguish. The process of destruction of the bank began when tongues disobeyed and eyes looked back into eyes of bankers. I am a woman of many tongues. One of them is a person. With my eyes I take the world out of its worldliness. The banker is a man whose eyes are steel and whose tongue is iron. The tongue of the banker is one among my many tongues. In my nature is a note that meets the image halfway down the street. I cannot be a banker. I sit on banks of a river and pun endlessly on words that go with moods of lovers. Food is the frame of mind. I call love my food. I live thinking of you. I think of you to make life real outside the bank in a neighborhood that threatens the existence of the bank. Life you are. My tongue calls on you. My eyes experience you with familiarity of sea that feels raindrops on its body.
That you are which I am not and
what will never be mine.

The rain speaks all languages. In the soul of my heart you are. You belong to earth before you are mine. The streets know the voice of a person in love. In the night of the diamond sweets were shared and sentimental lies told. Romantic love is war within a social order. Death waits smoking a cigarette in the room next to the bed on which I lie and ponder about rain. Our dreams never leave us alone. I look for that loneliness outside my dreams. Exiled from dreams I come closer to you. The woman, land and river compose the self outside dreams. It rains and the rain speaks. My love is a monkey on a green tree in spring. Capricious as a cloud is the heart. The poverty of romantic love is alienation of objects from beings. I look for you among objects. One sun. One moon. One fountain at the crossroads. One you. We are divided as two sides of the same road. On hot days this road turns into a pool of silver water. My heart goes down on the floor. On red floors I built dreams for you. My body struggled with age. Fate is a lion. I took birth at the wrong place in the wrong time. The right place in the right time is spring in Japan. I've never been there. I've heard from poets that white ground turns blue in Japan with the arrival of spring. In Akira Kurosawa's movie *Dreams* a society is portrayed in which the worker is artist and people do not age. The old dance in steps of young. Age has not taken away the child in them. Death, history and madness have unconcealed forms of sadness at the edges of language. The sadness that Japanese poets speak of is so different from sadness among poets of Middle East or India. With Japanese sadness is natural as hands of a poet. Among Middle Eastern poets sadness is cultivated as a discourse to compensate for pleasures of life or loss of paradise that sweet death can make possible. In India sadness is a condition of life. Poverty makes us sad as much as love or death of a person. The sadness of white ground turning blue comes from a certain philosophical tradition of Buddhism in combination with the social history of Japan. The evocative power of transitional metaphors has to do with seasons moving around one another forming circles with circumferences that reach out to the universe that in turn can be seen in a grain of rice. In his work Akira Kurosawa exploits this idea of infinite circles expanding within an infinite circle that is one among infinite other circles in conjunction with the humanist tradition of the West dating back to Marx and Shakespeare and before that Saint Francis and Socrates. The loss of giving leaves the world destitute. Redemption is awareness that another being's suffering, however small it may appear, is greater than mine. Men are born not just to die. Men are born because they are willing to throw away the cloak of masculinity from their bodies and cultivate the love of a mother for her only child. Life forgives itself for being life. I was never a romantic lover. I love you the way a child wants to be on borderlines blurring the distinction between culture and nature. I am not sad because I think that you broke my heart. My heart was broken the day I opened my eyes. I am sad because I miss you.

Boat Woman's Song

It took time for me to give my heart to you because I don't easily fall in love. Cities shrink to size of a peanut the second I realize there is no love there. In the sun is a yellow rose whose rays run through velvety hair of sky. As my eyes bleed I give my lover the gift of a smile she wants of me. She never asks for my heart though I leave it behind on her doorstep. Her feet touch my heart and the stain of red on her nails glitters in moonlight. Red is the moon of love. My eyes turn red with sleepless nights taking me in their arms. I am nothing in this world. The one that comes when twilight is ready to leave walks out before light strikes the face of disappearing night. I am a woman of nights. I worry for lovers who never return. Thoughts of spoken words impress upon their light hearts. I worry that lips of their hearts might turn dry thinking of desert nights when we stood as cactus plants with sand sweeping our bare bodies. I choose a lover who has an affinity for night. I give my body to one who gives me her heart. I take her body that takes my heart. My strength is in arms that work to live. I did not come to the world just to survive. I came into the world that I may turn the kiss of the bee on a flower into honey on lips of a lover. The moods of day are in my eyes. I forgive my betrayers after a rainy morning and wet earth bakes in slow fire of the sun. I could never make a boat for anything in this world. My eyes follow boats that go into the sea. I dream of flowers that dream of being touched by hands soiled with labor. I work with the joy of fondling a lover's body. My lover sleeps. She is exhausted by my touch. My still hands watch her dreaming eyelids. Flowers are my destiny. I give my lovers my destiny on dark nights. I try hard to stretch the day but it's never more than one dawn and one sunset. Wild is the sea as my lover's body. I measure time in seasons. There is one incomplete circle in which I was born. The other incomplete circle is when I leave the world. I take two incomplete circles and make one broken circle out of them. My life is all about broken circles. I make lovers. Lovers make me. When day comes to an end we are still broken. This brokenness I carry from the cloth I was wrapped in as a baby. Childless I made children in the imagination. Children of the heart are my lovers. Motherless they come to me. I am no mother of theirs. I laugh when they complain about fate and other women. I am earth that receives seeds of falling rain. I am a woman of sorts. I sort of forgive but I will not be taken for granted. Give me salt and let me have sunlight. I will give you love in return. Time the pendulum I have never taken seriously. Time is drops of rain that glaze my lover's skin. I kiss that body of hers. I taste time languishing on her body. It was the time of my life. My worlds are private worlds of shadows at bottom of seas. I am a part of a world induced to sleep by shade of trees. Shades and shadows. I am a woman among men. Among women I am a woman who is a person. I am a woman among women who are also mothers, wives, sisters and daughters. On streets I am a woman among women who do not fit anywhere in the world of men. I am a woman to the prostitutes whose arrival in history coincides with that of family. I am a woman proud of her lips. I speak and the world listens. I laugh and there is an echo that comes back as lightning to strike complacent streets. I dance and spirits walk out of hallowed place of cremation. I love and the heart of the world stops beating for a second.

Weekly Fair

I offer words as libation at the feet of the beloved. With water I drip your feet. With wine I touch your cheeks. With light I drape your body. Men who do not understand malign me. The dust of their anger covers my sight. Conflicts of all kinds set me on the run. In my compulsive attachment to dogs I learnt the art of wandering without an end in view. I write stories that do not anticipate readers. I make poetry without music. I compose songs that can never find the right tune. I cannot stop loving you. In this weekly fair where people buy and sell alone I stand watching nothing and watched by nobody. Time passes as if it is in the nature of time to pass. Literally time performs the role of a metaphor. What was time other than a metaphor of passing? I am worn out by illusions. The illusion that I am is worn out by illusions. I cannot forget the sweetness of a mango that I ate as a child with my head in the lap of a woman. Time did not affect me. I recognize faces in this fair. The weakness of men touches my heart. I must sing to speak my love. My song will declare your beauty to my soul that I may not forget the moment. The economics of love is in distribution of wealth. What is it I can give you that really means that I've given you? The hunger of my belly I give you. Can life be sweet in itself without another? I fell in love as a secret preparation for the arrival of death. I could not challenge time without paying the price for it. Could I give up my sense of possession and still be in love? One without a sense of possession is a lover of night. She loves but she is not in love. An alternate economy without buying and selling can be imagined. That is love that springs from matter without being controlled by matter. My things are yours. There are no things to be shared between us. My things are not mine. Things are things that are there. My love is a thing in the purest sense of the term. The pen that I hold in the profoundest sense of the term is an image of my love. Love is not mine to be taken. I am chosen by love that is spirit of matter. In the spirit of matter I love you. I will be gone, as matter will dissolve into spirit. You will not cease to exist. Will my blood give meaning to your existence? Will your eyes turn red at the sight of blood on the pavement? Blood does not go down pavements made of concrete. Economics is not an explanation for electricity you produce in my nerves. The magnetism of bodies belongs to aesthetics of the flower within the seed of a flower. Everything that I saw was the dark seeing through you into me. My words are not imminent. They are nervous and frail. I dedicate them to the maroon nail paint on the little toe of your left foot. My words that are real flesh and real blood are dedicated to a form. The forms live while my words die dutiful as soldiers obey commanders in throwing away their bodies in shifting battlefields. I am weak-willed. My love is beset with doubts. I was raised to believe that love is outside the material state. I am convinced that such a love is material in its deepest sense. In my oneness with you I experience that love. Material love. Life as consciousness is one particle in the becoming of the universe. The universe in its ultimate seclusion recognizes that bewildered particle. In you is the universe generous as lovers are at peak of passion. It would be improper if I walked into the weekly fair a mile from where I live and stripped my clothes and uttered syllables that meant nothing. I would be stoned to death following which my image would have a mass following. Property is death. To keep things is to take away the essence of things that things cannot be kept. The amenities of modern life are nothing more than amenities. Homes that are fixed in time and space are forgotten before noonday sun has passed away. I love you in the nakedness of my body in the weekly fair stoned by passersby that do not know me.

In March month of mourning I paint walls blue. March is not to be trusted. It looks like spring during some mornings. The heat gives me a headache. Bouts of cold strike my chest. For what does March mourn? Spring is spring because flowers bloom once in a year. The smell of spring in your breast. March mourns anticipating periodic loss of spring. I mourn loss of March at the height of winter. The sunshine in my blood mourns coming of spring with tears of joy. I weep for March as all true lovers. March is my lover for all March knows. The origins of life can be traced to March. The blood is fresh in March. Trees are nourished in martyred blood of March mornings. I sit alone dreaming of friendship and the hopeless abuse of lovers by their families and childhood recurring in dreams that tax my body. She is a flower in March from Japan. The subaltern woman is the most vulnerable of all flowers. March is a subaltern month. Spring is season of all seasons because it is season of the subaltern. Something in my blood is subaltern. I borrowed my language from discourses that belonged to Moors and Egyptians and Lebanese and Chinese and Japanese and Turkish. Every stolen word had the sound of March in it. I came home a tiger without prey but with a sense of direction. In the cave where I longed to rest my days I was a content tiger. With the ebullience of March she entered my room. I am a child of March. March entered the room and I declared my childlikeness. In March I was a woman in love. That was the loveliest March of my life when I flew with the wind. The currents of fate were all for me. When the clouds parted to let in the warm sun after a brief torrent of rain it was only to please my heart. For clouds to make this gesture meant so much to my love-stricken heart in March. Intricate were March-time intimacies. In March philosophy left the classrooms and confronted lives on streets. Philosophy became the street. The philosophy of streets that the subaltern voices in her moments. The streets of philosophy on which the subaltern lives her moments. Both are exaggerated views that March produces in lovers of streets. There are no subaltern lovers. Only subaltern non-beings. You don't call it philosophy.

Nor do you use the term subaltern. You stand at the threshold of a land that you are familiar with by sight. You may or may not be working on that land. The connection between you and the land is arbitrary. All terms that control the usage of land are changeable in time. If my words are relative to my situation I am not in a position to write about you without acknowledging that your situation is not mine. You are in a subaltern position to mine. I must subaltern myself in order to know what you feel like. If at all you feel

I know that you like roses in March. I must love that subaltern in you that I cannot approach. When land speaks to hands that have tilled it since the inception of agriculture that is the awakening of the subaltern. Was the subaltern asleep to begin with? Was she plotting the plot of March that would change the world? What is the world that changes? Whose world is it? My words confound you as much as me. You must be something that I love you. What is my love but March waiting for finest rose of the season to drop in your breast. The girl from Japan is a blue rose that does not exist in the natural world. It is an intimate construction of an intricate heart. Were it not for March I might have forgotten her face. Her face was intricate as March in the most intimate of seasons running through the third month of the western calendar. Where I come from March is not the word and not even spring. Warm summer stands at the door in the time that corresponds to March.

The month of flowers is the labor of love coming out of the body of the subaltern. Subaltern is the March of seasons and intricate are my intimacies with you.

When I move to another place I have only changed rooms. The rooms of the past keep coming to mind. Death permeates the language of memory. Memories that have nothing to do with death have nothing to do with life either. A palace of thousand doors and none of them open. That is not memory but a palace whose doors will not open except to the one who lives in the present. I crossed borders at night. It is a habit I picked up from a dream I dreamt as a bed-wetting child. I was standing on the tip of a pencil. I might have been praying to the mountain that stood opposite me. I was puny as a doormat. I could easily have been walked upon without any effort. I was praying for white rain. Sunlight struck my body down. The pencil shook. I was falling at the moment that pieces of my body dispersed in space. The sun was bloody and the universe was quiet. In the mountains the light was less than human. The ecstasy of sand that trembled when touched by light made me feel like a woman. Discourses broke down. The light and sand and me were the same entity. The sand danced in the hands of light. I was a particle of light in a particle of sand. I am a vagabond with delusions. I spoil the world with innocence. In the mouth was sugar that went down my throat. I wanted it to melt before snows of the mountain turn into waters of the river. I thought of coming back home. Home does not come toward me. I go toward home. I rejoice in the nothingness of my pursuit. I arrive at the radical conclusion that what I call love begins at the tip of the pencil that I hold in my hand. What comes before that is my hand that is inexplicably subaltern. I cannot pretend that subaltern is a term coined to refer to the subaltern. Love is what is produced by the tip of my pencil in the split of a second. Gone are days of melancholy. I see a note in the weather that says I must leave. Ironies rebound on walls of superstition. What is it in you that I want and that I do not want to change once I am in possession of it? Of late I have become a moody person. The joy of watching a moment pass before me is that of a child coming into the world. Does the child share the same joy of coming into a world of poverty and pain? The child does not make the same choice that I make in loving you. I am in the habit of using words that I've learnt. I cannot do without them. My love is limited to what I don't understand. I know the historical context of the word. I cannot put it in place when I refer to my feelings for you. When I say that I love you I only mean that I do not understand my feelings for you. I don't understand you and I accept to know the person I do not understand. You are a mystery that does not intimidate me. I am not broken at the thought that you might change and never be the same person whose face I memorized in the nerves of my finger. The world is full of mad people. I am one of them. In the madhouse light is a concept. In the light of madness I make gestures of love. My eyes are silent because I am thinking of you. Naked I entered the world. I love you as a persona. I was clothed under the sheets. I wanted to belong to something even if it was a piece of cloth. In the language of madness I find traces of a drawing made exquisitely with the tip of a sharp pencil. I was a child and the stars of night dipped their faces into the ocean that washed my feet with light.

Involution

Integral to life is being. A consciousness emerged from the chaos of universe and it happened to be me. I am just another context to be understood within a group of contexts. Did the universe make a decision before the point of my emergence into consciousness? Was I another consciousness in the states of the universe? A universe where time is not an issue except to the consciousness endowed with a body that can feel pain and look for the source. I was conscious of a wind from sea that did not touch the waves. I am written as destiny in the palm of your hand. Were you the wind that was from neither sky nor sea? It came from Japan the wind from a movie of Kenji Mizoguchi. Humanity that is deeply hurt is relieved through the balm of compassion. Silence succeeded all conversations that brought pain to the sender of the message as well as receiver. The silence of waves that are untouched by wind. The silence of wind that brushed waves with hands of a dream. The lotus smiled when a silent glance pierced it. The seer of the lotus smiled as well. Remembering a smile is to remember the rain of summer. Midnight and noon are partners in love. The nightmares of living with the dead never leave me alone. At noon and around midnight I was conscious of the smile integral to being of the universe. In quiet rooms we came to terms with the splendor of horses romping through evergreen forests. Mizoguchi has a way of dealing with sadness that reminds me of Nazim Hikmet the revolutionary Turkish poet. Sadness is a gift made for a world that refuses to be happy. The awareness that sadness can be given makes it beautiful. In that beauty that comes from a body beaten by vicissitudes of life there is a gift waiting to be given. The only real gift is what hurt could have made possible. The unhappy world is hurt but the gift of smile is withheld in the palm of the hand. It cannot give its sadness and therefore it suffers. I give you my sadness but you fail to understand the logic of sadness. There is a Telugu song that says that you must laugh in life as in death because once dead you cannot laugh anymore. The universe is there to be laughed at at all times. I laugh when I remember how you shuffled personae from that of a clown to a lover and a child. It was the magic in your expression that did the trick. The magic of the universe is that it does not experience the consciousness of being nothing. I do. The knowledge of my need for love is a profound reminder that I share in the nothingness of the universe. I was long dead before I was dragged out of my mother's belly. I woke up from sweet death. Love connects me to the universe I lost in the birth of consciousness. Life is sweet and it makes me sad to think that I am only a particle of fluttering consciousness in the sleep of the universe. I sleep only to know you. My waking is a preparation for the gift of sleep I give you. I am a slave of the suburbs. I am addicted to rains in neighborhoods where nothing works. Everything is cold and gloomy. Like the universe I am forgotten. I live in the forgetfulness that hurts my sense of who I am. I am nothing in terms of the universe. In the world of people I project myself as an idea to be recognized in the body of a lover. In your body is the soul of the universe. One grand sensitive magician is this universe. Your body tells me that I press my ear against your breast. I hear the breathing of the universe. I expected it to be quieter for all its dark passion. Magic is the power of compassion that can rouse the sleeping universe in the hearts of men who lie in ignorance. In you I realize the truth of the universe. My headaches are a sign of the coming of the age of boredom. You smile in a mock sadness as you look into my eyes.

Scream of Echo

My destiny is a dramatic performer. I am tears on the face
of the performer. If music must conspire to make me sad I
would still listen to it. My ear has a destiny of its own. So
do my tongue and eyes and nose and skin. They are
individual destinies at variation with one another. I follow
the destiny of the skin. Blind is my skin ready to touch and
be touched by darkness. Where there is a lack of anonymity
my skin will not glisten. My destiny is a thing of cities. I am
a villager at heart. Wherever I go I must look for a friend. I
search for silences. I listen to echoes of shrill birds that
animate the humdrum of cities. When we did not work we
talked. When we worked we talked about our work. We
also talked about nothing as we made love. At every mistake
of yours I look with pity. I am bored with my pity. You
don't mind the pity but you never accept the mistake as
mistake other than something that belonged to the situation.
You tell me how powerless you are when it comes to
situations. Your body is a situation. It needs to be
understood. I try and fail. The cities have taken their toll on
me. I am insensitive as my destiny is to me. I protest to live.
My protests reverberate against walls of my heart. My
hardened heart deserves to be broken. Music can drive it
mad. That makes my destiny a sad one. I am in love with
sadness which comes with being in love with you. I am a
dramatic performer. Echoes are illusions. I am in love with
dramatic illusions that my performing destiny creates for
me. Illusions are echoes of other illusions. My dramatic
destiny is full of such echoes. It pains me when you reject
my body. You are welcome to mock my destiny. The touch
of my skin I wish to be acknowledged. You can say no to
the sky. I want you to respect the falling rain. I am rain in

the dark. The destiny of my skin is in love with me. I can be touchingly naïve when it comes to using words. The mask of naïvety that my destiny uses when it smiles fools me. I submit to blindness of my skin expecting it to lead me. I don't want you to misunderstand me. Inadvertently you are a part of destiny. You were there to choose to be chosen by me. Our destinies are negotiated in some sense. That's what makes the event of my knowing you a dramatic performance. We are birds for all that I know guided by an instinct to find truth. The truth is in rain that falls on parched land. Was it destiny of land never to see rain before sun consumed the soil? The universe is without destiny. It goes. I cannot go on without believing that I had a destiny. If all choices are meaningless then the universe will last as long as I do. My death deforms the universe. The universe is deeply humiliated every time I explain to myself that I am destined to love you. How can I explain my destiny to you without alluding to the fact that I am a born liar. That is a universal truth. In the dream I am conscious of the dream that I am dreaming. I act with that sense of freedom. From a cliff I leap and fall on a floating cloud. Spontaneous as spring you come and lie beside me. My destiny is a dream that the universe constructed for me. Tired of being a performer I decided to go back home before age took me in its distinct jaws. My retirement was dramatic. I was at home with the universe. In you my skin hardened by time felt that it had found its destiny. Hunger taught me to respect food. The same hunger made me compose lyrics that could not be sung but were written into my destiny. Books offered me solace but life changed me. It was not a life filled with music. Only a scream that tore the universe into fragments. I heard echoes of the scream.

Turtles

I must give my heart before I give body. If your heart is
mine it does not follow that your body is mine too. You
preserve your body as if it had rights of its own apart from
your heart. I never thought of your body except at times
when it was so dark that if my destiny stood before me I
would not be able to see it. My heart carried your heart as if
it belonged to my heart. Who did my heart belong to if not
me. I was drunk with happiness before wine ever existed.
Either I burn the whole town or I am in love. Young I was
drunk with youth. In age I drank with a lust for life.
Happiness burnt the edges of my skin. I belonged as I
longed to be. Your body was a space with a minority
complex. It wore extraordinarily bright colors in order to be
noticed by streets. I was embarrassed at the thought of
being on a street with a body visibly outright. You were not
completely bemused by my bedroom eccentricities. We
clashed as truths that belong to heart decide to establish
themselves in the realm of the other. It is impossible to be
strange without being ironic in some sense. You were
strange when you gave me your heart and preserved your
body. I was ironic in giving my heart along with my body
without caring to dissociate one from the other. I was also
ironic when I missed the irony of your strangeness. To you
it was natural as daylight in Japan is natural to the Japanese.
The daylight was unnatural as daylight can be to one with
eyes that are on exile. A mystery called night saved me
from penultimate loneliness. Ultimately I would be so dead
that it wouldn't matter if you decided to give me your body
and not your heart. My heart is crammed with voices.
Dreams of rejection. My throat aches when I think of you.
I can deny you anything but not sweetness. My heart that

rose to heavens fell into mouths of turtles. Was it my heart that you wanted more than my body? I would've loved to give you my body. The pain of receiving a body without a heart would be too much for you. What is too less for me is that my heart is gone and my body stays behind empty as a vault waiting to be filled. I never understood your body and its nuances. Your body is a joke in a foreign language. I grasp the irony of not being able to catch the joke while trying to feel the sound effects. Turtles on sand crawl toward water faster than my imagination can feel meanings of your body. Our hearts are foreigners to each other's bodies. Our bodies are foreigners to themselves. Save my body from madness that came from watching the protruding heads of turtles while loitering at the seaside. Your body swoops on my heart like a vulture. I save the flesh of my heart for the mental health of future generations. In the battle of wits we became human and forgot the universe. Human love is a form of emptiness. Since when was emptiness with a form. Not perhaps since the beginning of the universe. The form made emptiness accessible to our hearts that conceived emptiness in the way we refused to let go of our bodies. I know the logic of this line. It ignores power relations. I am absorbed by heat of your imagination. Your body battered through centuries of oppression will not have it any other way. Absorbed by nights I turn into a castrated chimera to the delight of hyperactive children who will not sleep until late midnight. Fate is human because fate is passionate as the heat in which I burn. Your body is fate. I react with anger of a victim. I throw my heart far on the street close to the garbage can. My body grovels in dust. I pawn my body to pay debts that I have incurred in satisfying the self-same body. Give me a kind word that I may forget I ever knew you.

Blood of Roses

I can imagine suffering in store for one destined to forget
blood of roses strewn on floors of lovers who must return to
work before nine in the morning when traffic is at peak of a
climax it experiences each day at the same hour I am an
error who dresses like a dog my soul is overwhelmed with
images you pass through all of them like a thread through a
series of beads the image that is the closest to the breast you
are if there is something in nature that understands kindness
may the something take you in its arms and shelter you
from storms I had a ball with reality blanked out of
existence for a time being by the sky the inequality that I
could not bear in the city I had sought you as the door that
my life was capable of arriving at without feeling that I had
lost my appetite for outdoors I am full of you without the
terror of fullness obliterating the person that I am that's as
light as my body gets while in utter obscurity of my nature I
practice elegance at every opportunity I go back to the
village it is not just a question of roses but the background
that sets the blood racing down mountains your suffering is
real because your eyes have seen god I laugh at illusions and
illusions do the same to me suffering rose make me a
particle of your blood let me experience the spectacular
panorama of your body in your brain is the village that is
green all year along I walk in that quiet village in that part of
night after midnight I don't see the heavens the suns and
moons and planets closed to my sight it worries me to see
one shriveling grape in the shape of my body I divided my
life into parts my days belong to the waters and my nights to
land I was old before I was young I became young when I
saw a rose that flashed the image of a life at wit's end what
have I done to deserve the sunlight in my shoes the poem

without words is naked of the fact that work brings us
together the one without pages triumphs in joy of having
never been born I suffered as a rose and my blood is an
expression of this knowledge I resist the kiss of the dragon
that resistance gives me the power to persist in love with
my heart bleeding roses ceremoniously as if that were the
thing that hearts were meant to do which is to act a
preordained role that did not connect with what came earlier
and what was that but sleep and more sleep you are the
mistress of syntheses I court you as a rose the limited
language of a limited discourse throws me off balance I
travel ticketless in local trains I roll on pavements mad with
ecstasy I make senseless conversations only to be slapped
by a passerby disgusted at the sights of faces that never look
but always seem to see I served a purpose in letting the
magic of purposelessness break my fingers I taste beautiful
to cats that are not even hungry it's the blood of that rose
that is me that is singled out by the cosmos to prove that it
exists I was picked out of that can of nothingness by hands
of an empty will that knew how to clamor for potatoes the
soul is blue and the outcome of a precisely calculated
explosion that happened in a brain that lacks consciousness
and therefore depended to be willed upon I see the love of
god in your dark eyes the rose is my conception to the end
of October I give it to soldiers and flower girls I am a virgin
in disguise of a thief the rose is what I have lost in the bitter
sweetness of a wintry dawn when I longed for long drawn
out absences you arrived as if you were always there or
never it made no difference because the arrival coincided
with departure words were left to talk to words about words
while the impatient blood of rose licked the lips of night in a
horrendous slush that came down in time-bound memory of
a blade of yellow grass situated along
the banks of a pond

I do not love life less because death will come to me in the form of an axe in a corridor with a dead-end. When the body is tortured for hours and days or locked in a prison with no contact of light it rots away with indescribable sweetness. I wept for broken bodies as my pastime. Broken bodies could not weep for themselves. Too much pain had numbed the bodies. Butchered in parts and left to die my thoughts were vacuum. Before the war there was peace that looked like war. The peace with interminable contradictions seemed preferable to war that was a logical outcome of the strange calm of latticed windows. In the war we knew something was falling and it was not dust from a storm. In peace we fought the bloodiest of battles. The war was the last stage of peace. In times of peace I learnt the art of reading between lines. I couldn't care less being on the defensive. The situation stank of a lifeless atmosphere. The vacuum with thoughts flooding it. It was an age of vacuity. Nothing was easier than being nothing. In the company of likes we seemed to be a lot at home with each other. Our hearts did not stop burning. What had peace done to us but make us more lonely and restless. The war had never stopped. It had changed its face and color. Peace was a name that war had invented for another time. I cursed the mouth from where words came. Silence had the strength of steel that could break a body with the caution of arsenic in the blood. Torrents of unanswered questions raged across my heart. The world is given to me. You cannot imagine. A story once opened cannot be closed. When I feel too much I want to talk too much. The cloud had no attachment to places. Birds told me that you wanted to say so many things to me. I am not an object of interest anymore. The fields of war produced in me the energy of ironic expression. You are the beauty of my heart. Green is the moon of madness. Maybe I am unreal but I deserve to be loved with more than words. You were never attached to me but to images of me in the garden of innocents. I gave you up for the universe. I know you better since then. Through instants of successive passion we kept coming in and out of our senses. The smoke thins away into air. The air has no memory of the identity of smoke. I remember you as daylight remembers dark to which it succumbs with the passage of moments. Eternity is time extended to eternity. Locked in fires of impermanence I let dreams fly out of my eyes. I insisted on tracing you to a point earlier than the earliest. Life before life. Before my words there were no other. From a distance you were a girl. Your body was heavily nuanced as bodies of women are. I gave my heart to a form. You were impervious to feeling the way men can be when convinced of the rightness of a position. I saw the person in you. It was not a form. It looked straight into my eyes and captured my nuanced soul. I seemed to choose the captivity that I was not born for. It gave me the pleasure of certainty in the hands of a form. Ravaged I kept waking up throughout nights. With my power to nuance things I manipulated the environment. I broke down in the process. I had to break down that I may also break the will of my oppressor. The person was frustrated with my nuances and struck and used my language against myself. The body knows the contact of cold walls in the dim afternoon. I imagined the heat of my tears melting the wall. Hope can be as paradoxical as memory if all the wars of words that plagued our dusks could be put together and carefully written down on the barks of trees. Those wars were painless. The skin was intact. What broke down was a blood vessel that could not be healed. Imaginary war was likewise imaginary peace. Those dark lines inspired a part of my body to write.

Thirsty for Blue

It looks like dawn. It tastes like dawn. It feels like dawn. It is dawn. I am a child because I play with myself. If I were asleep in the arms of my mother I would still be a child. I could never come to terms with the spontaneity that you knocked at my door at a vague hour and it seemed that I was waiting for you. Something like that could happen only to a child. I liked the idea of my feet walking past graves. It brings out in me the humor of life. Multiplicity was my nature but I was one person concentrating on the ground when I saw the hardships of working classes. Early in life I discovered a door that connected my personal life with what I wanted others to know of me. I created my own keys to open the door that opened one persona to another. That took my youth away as in the cawing of a crow. The keys were not always the right ones. The doors of personae refused to recognize the keys. I had to start all over. The rest of my life was an attempt to reconcile conflicts that it was hard to believe existed in the first place. I had to seduce the truth while at the same time desiring to articulate it with all my self. The selves of my past stand next to my door. I try my best never to look at them. When I look I have altered my self. Lonely and lost I could be easy prey to ghosts. I said nothing to no one under no circumstance. My innocence was short-lived. I apologized for all things natural and supernatural. My prison sentence was not coming to an end. You were soul to me when I was water of a fountain. I was a child with you. Your eyes were a pair of djinns running in all directions. The dawn that came had a special significance for me. It symbolized your hair on a pillow when you are in deep sleep. If I looked back my feet would not move any longer. Mesmerized by the hair of night I was thirsty for the blue. With wings of pity I flew across barbed fences. Pity lasted as long as night. In day I had to be someone else. The breeze upset structures of the imagination. I existed because I imagined. I write letters to dawn praising the blue. I compare dawn to a pink tongue that salivates with my letters. Bitter rhythms are these letters filled with thorns of dilemmas. Thin are the lips of rain that descend on my skin at dawn as unexpected lovers. I am beside myself in that receding dawn of white sun that absorbs the rain into its belly. I was a devil of a child before I was an angel of a person. Living as a tenant under owners who could throw me out at half a day's notice taught me to fly away in the dawn. My incapacity to love is my incapacity to be a person. The person comes from her situation. What the situation gave me was not love but movement. With nothing to declare as myself how could I invent the word love. I begged and slept as I begged. Tired I gave up civilities associated with normal life. I ate when I could. I walked wherever. Food without salt was my life. Nothing was left of me but the child that walked out of her bed and saw through the window beside her mother's bed a brief glimpse of a carpet in air and the child knew that her body was fate and with the fate of her body she walked to the carpet in the hope of floating across sea of the dawn out of this world the lights of cities disappear into villages blue is the light of grass she picks a star from the cosmos and hides it in her navel that leads to the underground where sits a tortoise on which the world rests in that dawn that was a blue carpet on the body of nothing the child shared the absoluteness of night in the relativity of day she was a woman who bloomed into a child in a black and white photograph from a long time ago her face looked sad but that was light from a mirror hanging on the wall of the bedroom giving the impression of immense sadness.

The Gypsy and the Farmer

Bread in the belly of a lion. I had to take the bread in order
to wake the sun and make the soil wet with sweat
of nature's sweet body. The translation of subterranean
memories into moments of present happiness. I
transgressed and I wrote. I danced as I came to the last line.
I had written the lines of a dance. I was dancing all the while
I thought I wrote. My feet transgressed as much as fingers.
I did not have a mind of my own and I never thought it was
an issue. The feet mattered and the fingers. I relied on them
to pluck fruits from trees and swing on branches. Fevers
make me cold and my body begins to believe that I am
about to die. The land never sleeps but is fevered by touch
of a person. On fevered land the feet danced without end.
The dancer was a step in the evolution of the person. Did
my steps dance while I ploughed the land? I dance for all
happy memories. I could go down all of a sudden and talk
about your language that I felt was one-sided. Where was I
in your words? You spoke of I but it was not me that you
referred to. Was I at all there in those strange noises? I
thought of what I had been doing all along for you. We
went on journeys despite the pain. You hurt your body. I
suffered. It looked like I was writing as well. You wanted to
believe that I would dare my very body to destruction as a
way of being true to you. I implied the truth in gestures that
I would preserve this body of mine for everything. The
waters of night made us solitary beings. The lost
connections resurged. Our happiness was made of moments
standing upon moments. Soul mates. We dreamt of days
without nights. I took an inside look at things that interrupt
the brain. In a peculiarly analytical spirit the dreams began
to fall out of our days. The land had made me conscious of

who I am. This consciousness was not my own. In itself it was a cloud without the sky in the background. The land was there before me like the night. Was there something intrinsic to consciousness that resulted from land that made me think that I was always there? The land suppressed the transition of a memory. It was the dancer who emerged from the depths of land. She was bread as much as spirit. Our nightless days were stories of houses abandoned by people on the move. The dancers were turned into a minority in the eyes of ones who worked on land. As long as land concealed one form of oppression it remained a fact of life that another was in making to replace the older one. Once the hierarchies were established it was not a question of one person against another. It was a question of the kind of work that had to be done and the distribution of produce. The placards were sealed with stamp of officialdom. You danced and I thought that my words preconceived those steps. The night danced in my dark eyes. I was afraid because I had forgotten the taste of bread. I forgot that bread tasted at all. You are not possessive. You are obstinate and argumentative. I had keys to your heart. You cried and guilt made me collapse on my knees. I had to confront uncertainty of the dancer while I stored bread for tomorrow. The uncertainty made us naturally happy while I shared my life with yours. For you I hoped and in you I placed those hopes. Your heart was the feet of a dancer. I could never learn uncertainties that bound your heart. I talked to myself about you. I was aghast at the thought of leaving you to the winds. I infused the soul of wine into my letters. Did the idea of wine precede birth of the vine? You whined about unfairness of life. The drinker of wine was preoccupied with the ironic coincidence of meeting the planter of seeds. I wrote about suffering and I meant every word without exception.

A Foregone Conclusion

I get what you mean even when I don't understand you. In my loyalty to you as a friend I earn my freedom. Fate the mercenary stood aloof from my gaze. If the universe does not exist neither do my sorrows. A nameless condition is non-existence. I am a non-actor in a non-space. What is considered 'I' by none is an invisible string hanging to nothing. Time cannot destroy the unborn. Born I choose to love you. Otherwise I am a slave to freedom. The freedom to love you is freedom that comes from center of my eyes. The freedom that is given to body. My body uses freedom as if it were more than an idea. The freedom of body is language of flickering eyelids on the verge of sleep. What has my body done to deserve such freedom? My body wrote poems about bodies. The gods were there to rescue the body from imminent destruction. I choose to love the body as if it were you. I offer this body that is you to gods as you look with mock appreciation. Your soul is not one with the gods. I tell you how I feel about the prick of a needle. You think I am talking about the haystack. I am lost and so are the gods by your defiance of things. Let me free you of myself. I am not the kind that was ever in fashion. Think once that I am a persona in need of you. Lovers' minutes are infinity. The minute in which you are with me goes at an infinite speed. The same minute is infinitely slow when you are not with me. A cloud came toward a plant in a no-man's land. The cosmic darkness wound this spot called the earth in its bosom. Like the plant the earth responded with indefinable pleasure. We talked our way through time one minute past eternity. In the mirror I saw evening sunlight on the wall. Minutes later I noticed an absence. In the gap between sunlight and shade I discovered that I was in love.

Was I waiting for you who haunted my room like paint on a wall? You feel what I believe. The belt of passion whipping the breeze. Did the breeze relent to the alien language of passion? Calm was passion that exhilarated in the music of shadows. The dark was ahead of me despite my waiting for it in light. I looked under my feet and there was nothing. My eyes that waited for you refused to close. Closing eyes that meant death to life also meant the life of a universe that expressed itself through death. It was easier to die than live. The universe chose me for a lover. In return I made fun of the universe. The universe did not laugh. What made death different from life was that life was funny. Death did not know how to make faces. At some point in time I could not see any feet any longer. Sometimes waiting can be longer than life. My feet were light as air. I only saw air. Take your time because you will lie with me in the cave of night. The night was the lodge of travelers who had forgotten their way. We saw the world at night. Your feelings were in mine and my feelings were in eternity. One friend for a lifetime and one glass of water from the river to slake my thirst. I lived out unreality to the extreme point where the platform of a train station ends and life begins. I took care of myself in the sunshine before I counted the gray hairs on my head. The dot on my forehead is a star that I stole from the heart of night. The lover was a category apart from the rest of the sleeping world. She was before social life took the shape of institutions. Outcast because she begins a story with a foregone conclusion of the lover that strips the face of the mirror, she claps her hands in her room and echoes are heard in mountains. The preconscious universe knows her as the question that precedes the search for the origin of the universe.

The Turnip-eating Fanatic

If every corner has a corner to its credit then I am cornered
to believe that corners never end. I never looked at it that
way. I sat in the corner of an abandoned house and dreamt
of ghosts with abandon. I like jokes that show the joker
with the most serious look possible. In celebration of a
minority I made a garland of words. My thighs are sticks
but my lips are lustful. Friends and lovers make sense of the
universe. I create you in a thought. I am recreated in a
feeling. From nothing all of a sudden you turned me into a
writer of songs. Thank you for the roses that you never
gave. I took a sample of your sweetness and went home to
sleep. My bed is a virgin. I am a tiger from woods adjacent
to the lake where buffaloes cool their bodies against the
summer heat. Sugarcane is sweetness of my love. Beauty is
in the gesture of one who creates the gesture. As a child I
was a root that stayed underground. That's how I escaped
mortality of leaves and flowers. I envied the slenderness of
the stem. Brown as a bark I let sun into my skin. One day I
was a flower. I froze and mellowed alternately at the
thought of being held by a hand. I laughed as I died. That
sudden burst of life that you see in the dying I experienced
as I bloomed in warm air. I floated as fragrance across seas.
I took nothing of you before I left except the memory of a
gesture that I call my own. When you laughed it seemed
that you were born laughing. I was bitter toward you when
I was bitter to myself. When I was sweet I continued to be
bitter to myself. I loved the bitterness that brought me to
touch the life of a flower. Irony took the shape of a lion's
face. The father who lost his child returned home. He wept
as children do when they do not find their way back home.
He knew that things were not in the habit of concluding

logically. The mother in her being looked for alternatives. In separating the baby from her self she experienced the pangs of separation. It was a prelude to death. The chorus of autumn leaves that colored the ground knew that the ending of a song in a devious manner brought time to a halt. Age set in before age. In a vision I was that child. I knew the tears of the father the way I knew the bosom of the mother. I picked a fallen leaf and tore it to shreds. Mourning became a way of life. I went back to eating sugarcane. Too much sweetness was not for my soul. I became a fanatic turnip-eater. I was sick of home though the idea in itself never seemed unappealing. The heavens of earth like mirages keep a distance and stay where I am not. Hell is everywhere that I am. Our last moments are lizards that run in strange ways. It's hard to catch them. I was a turnip-eater before I was a fanatic. Turnips turned me into a fanatic. The incredible relish with which I ate them brought tears to eyes of girls in love. When I see you approach me the heart is full. It stays that way until every shroud of every body laid to sleep in the ground has joined the soil to assume another form. Bangles in sunlight. Turnips and more turnips. The truth is more than my using the word 'love' for you. My love is the truth that every turnip-eater knows. Fanatically speaking I have made the choice of turnips over sugarcane. Turnips burn the tongue. I am a born burner.

Burning was the condition of my body and soul. In sugarcane I was a friend to every bird and beggar that my eyes looked at. I was overwhelming in sweetness. In the juice of turnips I was lava of a dormant volcano. I hissed with fervor and rambled clumsily over villages and ponds. Turnips ejected the divine out of my humanity. I cannot say that you are unnatural when I am myself so unusually constructed. You held your soul with such fierceness that I knew I had no alternative but to devote my nature to eating turnips. Sacrifice is an act that the actor conceives in the process of letting the curtain down. I sacrifice eating turnips for you.

Rice and Red Pepper

I slept like a ghost when I had nothing else to do. The ghost
became human when it was hungry. I used a book as
appetizer for sleep. When the book did not help I was
hungry for a plate of rice with red pepper. The rice was
boiled to be soft so that it would blend easily with red
pepper. Salt was already added to rice while it was boiling.
Hunger can make stones palatable. That is the beauty of
hunger. In the end all differences are nominal though not
for the hungry one. Even the notion of an ending was quite
nominal. Work that occupies the body adds a quality to
hunger. In places where I am not considered a body worth a
second look I could eat anything that remotely looked like
the touch of food. In a way it made me believe that
everything lived at a more imperceptible level. I never
believed that I had a will. I thought I had a heart. Somehow
the rains always poured in mountains and not the
downtowns of cities. The cities that raged with heat as a
matter of routine were hungry for showers. The mountains
drank away the waters. Dry clouds made us nostalgic for
the sea. Meaning is a condition imposed upon language. I
mean that the hungry do not look for meaning. Rice with
red pepper is revealing. It means I am a person with no
taste. I am tasteless when it comes to everything except
hunger that comes from work. This hunger looks for no
answers. It is mysterious as a pearl that does not know that
it is a pearl. The neck that wears the string of pearls knows
the mystery of pearls. The heart that does not see a
difference between a pearl and a pebble discovers that pearls
are charmless catastrophes that mean nothing to a cave
dweller. I came to lonely cities and went back to lonelier
ones. Between dream and reality is the smell of sandalwood

dust. Weather, women and sea. I am fond of uncertainties. I could have been a sailor. I weathered the motions of sea. I was a woman who sailed carefully through uncertain passages. The uncertainty of passages with more than one meaning could not spice a life that ate rice with red pepper. With a spiced tongue I made love to mountains. Mountains responded likewise. Wet with rain the rocks of ages fell within the scope of my tongue. Old as imagination is the imageless stone where light impinged upon dark. Life was the outcome of the illogical. Seekers of miracles know better than to forget that rice with red pepper is miracle of all miracles. Rice is not a symbol nor is red pepper. A rose is a symbol. A symbol is aesthetic and what cannot be symbolized is the political. Symbols wear my body. I cannot eat a rose except with eyes. My eyes are tired and need to sleep. Hunger refuses to let me drift into sleep. The world is a rice field in a dream. The sky is turning red as red pepper. My tongue speaks of the coming of a storm. I do not want to leave this dream. I see dark wings floating against an immensely red sky. My tongue craves for redness of the peppered sky. That is when my shirt rebels against my body. I let my shirt fly through wind of the windows. How could the stone have existed without an image? The same way that image can exist without the stone. An image apart from object is not an image. An object that relies on image is one without a defining essence. Objects are images. Images enslave the properties of objects. Rice with red pepper is an objective condition. The senses are images of the belly which is the object. Rice sustains the belly along with red pepper. Who cares if the stone is imageless or not. The image of rice is derived from its being an object of the belly. Red pepper is the component of pleasure that is given to eating rice. In loving you I find the joy of eating rice with red pepper.

I am entitled to flowers on days that I don't stretch my body to let the sun come into my home. I am entitled to suppose that all that my eyes can take belongs to me. My eyes cannot take me therefore I am not mine. That was curious reasoning to prove that I am yours. I am dispensable on spring days when ten thousand things worry my head. I was in Arabian Sea and my mind was in Bay of Bengal. Of the moon for night is my loyalty to you. You became one of the gods and I your court dancer. If you called a red pencil blue it would start writing blue. Fate does not second what I first. In every language I learnt there was a woman as attachment. You had movements of a belly dancer in your responses. I slept in imaginary arms of a real friend. I woke up with a sensual headache that meant disaster for rest of day. While your body is still I can make the hair of your eyebrows dance. With you I walked on a long bridge that terminated on a point that I could not see. At the thinnest point of the bridge I felt intense need for expression. I must have been pregnant because I felt it. The first time I was pregnant I felt it and I was pregnant. My eyes that look are not real because they do not feel rain on the lids. It is a lonely heaven I must enter where my friend is not with me.

I renounce illusions of heaven and move into hell of realities. The need to defecate words was the side effect of my pregnancy. In utter modesty I exclaim that I am in the dream of every woman. Young I had the heart of a stone. I indulged in the joys of anonymity. Age brought me closer to the stick. I wrote celebrating what I believed was ageless. At all times I waited for one to arrive. That one who would break the bones of my body and feed my flesh to vultures. I waited with a sense of pride that you see in a bride about to enter her new home. Pain would numb my body that life may leave it without any effort. In the desert I was at home with sand. My heart does not wait for you any longer. It knows that separation is not in the nature of sand. We flow as dunes from one crescent to another. Decadence muted my imagination. In prison I saw the head detached from body watching moans of a suffering soul with irrepressible joy. My imagination pounced on my wrecked soul. The prey had responded to a natural instinct in the hands of the tiger. It went down without any feeling for the dramatic. The tiger had no idea that in its clutches was a prey completely at its mercy. The faces of the tiger and the so-called prey were predestined. In your hands my body looked for lost lights of a fatal imagination. There were no old lockers to be disclosed. It seemed that I was acting when I saw a body raised to skies and it seemed so like my own it did not seem that I could either sing or dance it seemed I had a talent for multiplying differences with similarities leading to dissimilarities and indifferences what did not seem was more to point than what seemed sunlight seemed to make the show but it was the night that spoke the world seemed to go round on its own but you were orbit of the world it seemed that I was dying of loneliness that was just a dryness in my breast that made it seem so I never imagined that I could be acting in a dream it seemed so myself that I was certain I had no other self reality was in the seeming and not the being you seemed to be in a sticky mood and I felt stony seeing you like that but your sticks were stronger than my stones they were tongues that lashed with venom and caused more damage than the cyclone the stick of your hand broke the stone of my heart I seemed to believe for the time being that it must be sunning stones at the same time that it rains sticks I seemed to sleep with you in a tent stolen from a caravan on its way to the sea it seems

that one loves things that are not understood in words
which is how you smile in the dark and I can feel it in my
blood that sticks like a stone to the lid
of a flying jug.

Wordless Pages

Write to me moments in a manuscript when the writing hand might as well not be making love to mirrors in gardens. Wordless are pages of the manuscript that does not speak to itself. The clock moved to December and I was still in July. Before the calendar was born I was a woman with all moments for my own. Inferences blew in the direction of wind. I inferred that the wind was white because clouds kept projecting strange faces. Today was great because I was congratulated for my long ears that touched the earth while I walked to the bazaar. Bizarre were those days when I was a banana in the busiest part of the bazaar. I inferred that I was gossiping about my best friends. A child ate the banana and there was a bonsai in the belly. The penchant for distance was in roots of my belly consciousness. I am an outcome of the belly. In the belly of earth I found the diamond of my choice. It was green as sunlight on sleepy afternoons. I wrote what I saw and what I saw was unwriteable. Is it because my thighs are dark that I must wait for rain to wash the soil of my unwashable feet. With the wealth of words I built a fortress of illusions. I entered the kingdom I created with hands. I am happy to be unhappy when I am not with you. My hands were on holiday when my eyes cried for joy. I was affected by you. I changed myself. The sea sleeps but not the fish. The light of night vanished in the night of lights. It was darkness and there was nothing to vanish. In the night of longings I was a prisoner of birds. They pecked my eyes for sheer pleasure of watching me laugh at the sight of blood. I rose with curtains of a window that touched the heavens. Was I a girl before I was a child? Are all seeds potentially plants? I will never understand nature's sense of humor. Through birds I learnt that my body could fly. Through my body I learnt that birds knew the language of flowers. Through flowers I learnt that my body had the semi-solidity of boiled potatoes. One star is same as another. One night no different from other. Time does not exist if I don't make it go by. The river of misfortune dogs the waiting lover. I waited for the sun to go tired of its shenanigans with light. Hankering for bread I multiplied the steps that my feet took with the number of times that my hands moved. From the total number of movements I subtracted the number of moments that I waited for you. I inferred that the page was born before the word. On pages that had no words I made declarations of love and honor. That did not alleviate my hunger for softness of boiled potatoes. I turned waiting from a theme into a way of life. I was desolate with the image of you in my heart constantly reminding me of you. I did not let the image go. It was more than you at times. When you entered my room I felt that you were just standing outside the door waiting for me to open it. On steps outside my house we kissed for life. The steps dissolved and we were back to nothing. How can a word be poetic without a past attached to it? In that past when we were far from knowing one another those words did not fluctuate in spaces as roses do when the eye does not look at them. You entered my life and words turned into poems. The waiting was wonderful because I waited for nothing. On pages of nothing my love for you is inscribed in iron for eyes of jealous readers. A passing thing such as time will not break me. I was not breathing until I heard your voice. I breathed while at the same time I suffered the loss of your presence. I might be dead with memory of your absence causing me suffering. I see you and all moments change to nothing. We move swiftly through time as wordless manuscripts are caught in currents of an intelligent destiny that recognizes faces of nothing.

Evil Eye

I go to bed with your name on my lips. My lips wake up
with the sound of your name on them. If you could read my
lips you would be able to read your name on them. I am
slated to agony by a force that is outside me. It does not
exist. It originated in the plate of passion. I fight it with the
might of my insight. Have we turned from friends to
strangers now that you know my passion for you. It knows
you and it knows me. This strange demon that mimics
passion and turns it into a farce. I renounced devilry for
artistry. On sands of the seashore I developed the tendency
to be religious. My chest burst with phlegm unable to
control smoke from entering the nostrils. I strolled
recklessly into uninhabited places with carefully manned
borders. A soldier had a gun pointed to my face. It was a
blank smile that looked into his eyes. I virtually slept with
lights on that you may not pass by without noticing that my
heart refuses to sleep even though my eyes are closed.
Things get clear when lights are on verge of turning off.
That is the way with things. I refuse things. If I died for
what I thought was an illusion does that make my life an
illusion. I waited the day for a moment that did not wait for
me. Heartless was the moment with a pungency that could
make me cry without tears. These conspiracies that came
out of nothing turned me into a maniac for meanings. Is
there a distributor of profiles hiding at that no-point where
the sea pines for sky. I chose the profile of a distressing
lover. I did not write to change the world. The world would
not let me change aprons for eyes. A thing had to be a thing
and the eye that perceived it could change its perception of
the thing without a nod of apology. I was an apron before
your eyes. Your perception of the apron wore out with

wearing out of the apron. I felt your body and your hands long enough to see the slide show of your changing perceptions. The pain is past. The present is a flow of rhythms. Whistling and parroting the worlds of an organism I bore the weight of your gross insensitivity. You had the gun in your hands and I had eyes that could see the blankness of the world. In the slumber of ages I slept under rocks of eternities. I am awake because you touched me as dawn touches the wind. When I fall in love it is a life condition that I encounter. The complexities that surround your life are not you. Love makes everything an illusion except loving. Illusions are made of real walls. They do not go merely because I do not want them. I am a will of clay. I can be broken easily. Without the evil eye what am I. I cannot be a lover if I've transcended fate. I can be the universe which I am in moments. I am a lover because I comprehend evils of the eye. The madness of soul is response to any condition that cannot change on its own. I loved because there was a price attached to it. I paid it with remarkable docility. The truths of my life I discovered in never-ending tunnels and not in light. I had glimpses of what was neither evil nor the eye. It looked like fate but was not fate. I was not fated to know it either. In the oneness of soul I deciphered the symbols of anonymous eyes that threw masks with an amazing fury that enthralled my beating heart to stop beating. Death was the knowledge that my soul secretly aspired to. I experienced that knowledge at all times that I waited for you. You divided your soul between the world and you and me. I was your heart that pumped the blood to the rest of your being. I was necessary but not important. I saw the world differently from the one you saw with your eyes. Our destinies were in a state of perpetual conflict. Your eye prevailed over my heart. The world prevailed over you. Evil entered the eye of my heart.

I hurt to the point where you were forced to suffer my absence. Sunsets were long and there was no hope of the coming of night.

When Shutters Are Down

I am a lover with no condition not even human. The gypsy
in me will be dominated neither by nature nor other men.
Rivers have a way of disturbing my humanity. I feel
conditioned by moments that I am with you. Headaches
have a way of wiping out shapes of my imagination. My lips
can barely utter a prayer. The moment has a spur to it. It
bleeds but refuses to run. I am in pity for moments that
stand still and suffer. My body learnt the language of your
body on a cool floor in hot summer. Mirrors of mad
meanings were your bodies. One of them chose me for one
moment one night when one star I could see from one
bedroom one voice too soft that is yours one life for a
rebellion against one that mocks from a distance what is one
alternative to one desire in one weather when green is
yellow and white is brown once I looked into closed eyes
one proof I required from them that I was all theirs that one
time was enough for one to die of happiness for nothing
kills one like happiness does one know that in you is
fountain of my happiness you are one who can make my
lips suffer the noise of traffic made me think of one day
when my name will outlive me into those myriads of other
names that are written in same letters as mine that one day
of my one name I give you as if it were mine in the present
I was one bird in a lonely sky and one child on top of a
mountain looking at the world with one closing eye you
were one with my imagination I thought of you and my
thinking process was one with you I could make no
distinction between the one you were and my one self I was
near you in my one self I triumphed in oneness when I
realized the moment when I was you one death I had to die
in order to live as you that was one time I was a searcher for

truth that billions of stars were not equivalent to one nail on your little finger this one life was an accident entirely disconnected from rest of the universe the principle that things must pass before they can actually be one bangle turning into the sun the resilience of the tiger to enter the cave forgotten by time the odds against which the tiger had to function with a sun glaring like a bangle in a furnace that one tiger romping down slopes I am that's one perspective on life that comes with setting of the sun nostalgia is not about going back to spaces I knew in other instants of my life nostalgia is about evenings on a holiday when shutters are down one soul recognizing its formlessness the leaf at the tip of topmost branch ready to fall is the same as the root that lives in a state of death buried beneath the ground dead to eyes of a formalist alive I am rooted in the bottom of your being the source without any sources fanned by elements delectable is my body carefully baked in the oven of my mother's womb for nine long months normally born I was told in the year of the sheep of the Chinese calendar I am perverted by the size of juicy melons my tongue is redder than my soul I lisp as babies do and run toward melons I fall and cry I regress to times I was not conscious of a self I am a woman in my dark thirties I appropriate identities for my own I steal lines as I steal hearts from enemies my eyes welled up in tears when I saw floating populations I wondered if there were homes waiting for them I regressed into states of nostalgia as the shutters went down I was one with the world before I became myself I had to love you with no purpose but to love you the worlds I had to confront in you the smell of jasmine cannot be contained it escapes through softest pores before it touches clouds and descends on dry hills as sweet rain from the little house in the village I experience the trickling music of running water I dream dreams where I am in that moment between life and death and one with one.

Intrigued by Daylight

In a perpetual state of waiting I became a dancer. I waited as
I danced. It was only a dance of words. Intrigued by
daylight I was also a worshipper of stones. I danced as if I
worshipped. I waited in that state of dancing. What did I
want from beings that I waited for with no feeling of
desperation. I anticipated life would come to my door. It
was daylight that intrigued me as it stood outside my being.
Transparent windows in a desert seized my raving
imagination. A dot of calm on which I stood as I waited for
you. Flurried by a filament that rocked my eyeballs I looked
for the intelligence of a being without name. What are the
motives of a lover who cannot confront the eyes of dark. I
was revitalized by fate that detested the sparks of white
glistening in my hair. Crisis upon crisis devoured my brains.
Madness was a thing of spirit. The gallery I dreamt of did
not have a parapet. My mother's hand came out of the
endless well of dark and tried to hold me. She could not and
I started falling. I made the connection between
remembering and forgetting in awareness that I did not
belong to myself. Kiss me sweet that I might forget myself.
My body is in love while my soul prepares for an
unexpected journey. A private song sung in the midst of
silences. The tables are made of the dust of splitting lights. I
was intrigued by fire coming from the nostrils. It was a
fever that made me think of mother. I danced because it was
daylight and I could be seen by the sun. I regretted leaving
home before completion of the dance. Home was a feather
that I saw in the shattered mirror of a school bus with no
children in it. Reality turns me on when time is on my side.
The king of serpents is the secret father of the hero in the
story of the lone child who grows up to be a lover of

animals. The mother functions in absentia. I tore into the breast of the serpent king. I plucked the flower of the mother from his belly. I rose to eternity before I fell back in time. My hair was black and my eyes were burning. The lands on which my legs walk are all mine. They became mine in the process of the run. My sweet legs. They burn with fever. My eyes are in love with my legs. My sight is faster than my feet. I see the rose on top of the hill before my feet can reach it. My legs have suffered intolerable humiliation of being second to eyes. They rebelled and protested as I entered age. My inconsiderate eyes continued to mock my suffering feet. Disgraced my feet decided to go down. Their attachment to eyes kept them going. You are my eyes. I run for life each time I wake from sleep. That intriguing life in the mind of the microbe. I need to be overhauled because I keep going back to spaces that reject me. I hate flowers though I have the feeling that flowers reciprocate with longing. I construct flowers when I miss daylight. I am a girl whose thoughts are dedicated to flowers. Thoughtless I began the discourse of overhauling myself. I came to a point where the tunnel seeemed to come to an end and there was no light. You won my heart with innocence that inspired in me feelings of murder. I murdered the light that I never saw. Used to dark I turned darkness into a way of life. I was a leftover from last night's dinner. Call me a towel or a hand that wipes wet lips. Tears devastate me more quickly than storms. I am neither forgiven nor understood because I neither asked nor deserved a look at the rising sun with its immense capacity to watch struggling wills rise and fall with the same treacherous determination of a painting on a wall that can just be there even after a bomb has destroyed the entire neighborhood and there are a couple of old men who collect remains one of which is the painting that is intact and

evokes the serenity of the sun as it stands outside the world
of men and women projecting a demeanor
that is childlike.

The Day the World Stopped Turning

I stopped the day I could not comprehend the functions of objects in the natural world. Could the flower exist without you to compare? I related my feelings about a lake and your response was cool as waters of the lake. I diverted the mystique of the lake toward you. Did it matter whether the lake existed for me to make the comparison? You might never see the lake until the day the world stopped turning on its axis. The lake would still be there for me to make the comparison. The lake exists because you do and not the other way round. Infinite and one is my love for you. I prefer the thorn to the withered rose. The thorn has the perfection of things that have not come into this world. The flesh submits to demands of the thorn. Elegant and outside time the thorn can look at withering flesh with the detachment of closed eyes. My world falls in shade of two eyes. One in dawn and the other in twilight. I flirt with the possibility of turning the tables against time. I propose to do that by colliding with stars at night. That would be a sign of inveterate light-headedness. A revolution that ignores the power of fantasy is destined to be forgotten. Turning in my own world I spoke of revolutionaries as fantastic animals. I was fantastic until I came to a lake with no fish in it. How could I not wait for the one I love even if the bluest of lakes had to turn dry as an untouched bowl. Lost among the lost and found in presence of a lake I was born to hate mathematics. I could not help admire the austerity of the thorn. It suited my suffering flesh. The thorn was mathematical in the precision with which it pressed upon wounds of the flesh. I roared as a dying tiger in a cave. Children sleeping in wombs of mothers in the village outside the forest woke to echoes of my cries. The unborn understood that I envied their state. Like the lake in question the moment of parting was waiting for us. I thought I had words. Words said nothing. I was speechless and retrospective. I started feeling dizzy the day the world stopped turning. The spells of dizziness made me weak. I missed the time when I was not born. Can one soul exist in two bodies. Can two bodies exist as one soul. I stand like a book in dusty shelves of a public library waiting to be opened. Make love to my soul before you touch my body. I want you to experience the fragrance of the bower before you arrive at it. I feel the sweetness of destiny in your body. The time of revolution has come when your body will descend into the lake of delight. We prolong the joys of waking early by watching stars hide in the greater light of day. Did we ever sleep in the first place? Somebody's eyes must tell me who I am. A person's last romance has the beauty of an empire in its last days. It is a romance whose failure is written on its forehead. Decadent and wild the poets of this period are sentimental before their time. The leaves glow with greenness of things ready to die. I share the sentimentality of this moment. Lakes move before eyes. Revolutions are filled with bodies of men and women energized by light. The multiple climaxes of one single moment. The empire falls. I live through the fall. I loved you and not an idea of you. The aesthetics of decadence is words that take joy in words. A body is an object of the aesthete. I am the body of the aesthete objectified in the mind's mirrors. You are my most unique self that can exist outside of me. My unique self is not mine. It is the shadow of the word that hides within the object. I am a trespasser looking for meanings in objects. The object of my life is to enter the sea of unknowing. In another birth I will take the form of soil and you will be roots of a plant whose branches shade the faces of travelers going on journeys without ends.

My love is eternal but understand where I am coming from. The acquisition of sensitive details is a way of reproducing moments. Once I tell you something the thing changes. I tell you that red roses are eternal and they wilt and fall the very moment. My words turn gray once you touch them with your ears. I must be eternally young to produce words that refer to eternally warm days in spring. I am not certain if you were listening while I spoke about the rightness of things and the lovable that stood on ramparts of the desirable. Love occupies the brain when a million other things fail. The material world recoils with anguish at insipid idealism. Objects lure me into positions where I am struck by an invisible hammer on the back. I didn't know I was something until a stranger told me that my breath reminded him of a block of ice that he had eaten as a child. My words were cold in that instant. The word knew that the world was only a word. Did the world know that the word was a world. Void was the world of the word. Devoid of meaning I entered your soul. Silvery are my slippers and golden are my feet. You mistake my slippers for feet. I mistake your home for your soul. The fragrance of your soul is in your home. You vacated the place and left the fragrance within me. I am occupied by voice of a ghost. When the radio is on I hear the ghost speak from a distance. Sentimental frivolities correspond to sinister slogans. Death gives me solace from windows that refuse to close. Summer's rain belongs to summer. My mouth is sick and I feel ignored as a rotten potato. I don't belong to summer. The rain is mine. I appropriate it from the corner of my eyes. On the day I leave this earth either it is raining or I am thinking of you. In analyzing a dream I arrive at the language of order. Young I suffered the loss of being wanted. With age I knew that too much of love meant the opposite of joy. Accept me for who I am and I am a water balloon. What would I be without dawn and twilight to redeem my sensibilities. Pictoriality brought sweetness to unseen images. What I envy in a culture is its ability to produce examples. In the kingdom of my heart there are no hyacinths. Suffering hounds me. I look for you in the loveliest of nights. That night was far from me. The music of illusions rings in my ears. A ghost that knew the bitter aroma of camphor liberated me. In a poem I look for a song. In a song I search for silence. What happens to my sanity in afternoons that my eyes are wet with happiness. Ten times I called your name and the eleventh time I saw you when my lips were sealed. Did you feel that I had reached my wit's end some time when sparrows were ready to wake me up. I never thought sparrows were worth counting. I woke up wondering if sparrows would notice that it was a stage with no audience. I acted my guts out to communicate my emptiness in words. I tasted the madness of love before I tasted honey. I pictured you as a cloud. I was rain that filled your emptiness. I am manacled by pictures of centipedes. I created a tunnel for you in my heart that connects to the brain and hands. A bird escaping from translucence of twilight entered the tunnel. Darkness wept at the sight of the bird.

Who knows how long I persisted in nothingness of the tunnel. You are not a person. You are music. I am words of the song. I need a haven for my stinging soul. The heavens smiled roses upon me. For you I rejected the gift of heavens. What is the being of a bee? Can the bee be? Is it in spite of itself? If I could be the bee I would be one with fewer words than what are locked in my chest and coming out as phlegm. On a spring day I rewarded myself with a rose. The madness of art is the soul sick with smell of roses and throwing out phantoms of sinister slogans in sunlight.

Insincerely Yours

I am a jackass of a stylist. Bitter and sweet more sweet than
bitter this was my time was I given the time did I take it
from a source that goes all the way to paradise I took a train
to the end of the world I returned by foot that I could revisit
forgotten landscapes I have been given with the mind the
awareness of your feelings for me things ran over my body
with speed of light I could not bear the thought of going to
bazaar where forms are merchandized as figures I
prefigured the form of a white ray of sunlight that pierced
the center of a loaf of bread the bread had no center like a
river it turned into formless blood all my life I was haunted
by a desire to forget what in fact I struggled to remember
when I was not in love I dreamt of writing the writing took
place in a dream even now as I write I am not sure if it is
not a hand coming out of a dream and penning these words
this hand will disappear as if it never existed back into that
dreamless state from which it arose as a dream like a lotus
from a pond our dreams are solitary as our lives I was in the
habit of emptying my soul of all content before I fell in love
I began things as if it were the first time I suffered I
remembered I changed once a ghost left the passages of my
soul's memory it never returned I had no expectations in
my soul your voice was an image I measured things in
terms of 51% and 49% because I liked the idea that what
made the difference was one percent we played a game of
silences I dispensed with a passage from memory I rejected
certainty with the very force that I needed it to the exile
homelessness was as natural as home my soul had two
mirrors in one I saw the other which of the images was
really mine I never knew the smiling rose and the dancing
heart rain was beautiful in life and necessary in art my

imagination is tired of fading rhythms my silence felt the
meaning of your silence you wanted me to speak and I
thought you were tired of language our conversation
abounds in inexplicable ironies I measured my words in
spaces my spaces I contrived in the dark sexual flowers in
sexual midnights with the prowess of a cat I saw through
the fabric of dark attachment in a sea of emptiness did I
reach the absolute when I walked into a lake I prayed to
nothing when I had to bless my friends the same nothing
that brought me into this world as a non-visual learner of
things perceptions change within moments the moments
stilled in white spaces it must be that all perceptions are
kites that want to touch the sky in the end they fall these
kites that roam uncertain of their past baffled by the breeze
in love with the lair I am insincerely yours a stylist to the
end though I could never intellectualize suffering without
attaching to it a sense of protest if I cannot forget not to
remember God it's because I cannot forget not to remember
God on a sable terrace I mourned for a mirror were they
tears on the face of the mirror I wondered I pressed my
cheeks to faces of shadows I turned into a shadow because I
thought that it was easier to be a receiver than a giver I
stuck the knife to the wall in the other room I hear noises I
long for personae when I am with one of them I jump to
the radical conclusion that the only operating mode of
reality is that of fantasy my father was a horse I rode upon
the dreamers of nothing are nothing in fact themselves
trapped in the utter insincerity of style they rise like foam
and fall to the beat of the returning tide in the gloomiest
part of night there are fishes that dream of me and curtains
that are whiter than snow the period of history I'm
fascinated with is when the artist learnt that stones could be
turned into works of art stones entered my brain I went but
my name remained in letters of stone whatever the

circumstances I understood music without knowing
the possibilities of rhythm.

Did I play the role of the lover and I wasn't yet in this world
I did not know you but you took me for grass on the
pavement I was a colorless tube from which water flowed
dim is the complexion of jealous eyes. It wasn't a dream. It
just wasn't real. History that defies the existence of God
also defies its own existence as history. The thought of
betrayal is sweeter than the action. The lover betrays in
order to love. I lost years of my life in unresolved dualities.
Sweeten me for I am summer's child. I want to be eaten like
soft rice with lentil soup that is given to children. I lived in
stories where the untranslatable moment was original as a
fingerprint and it was not a word. Why me I thought as if
posing for a photograph the camera had a logic of its own
distinct from the intention that my face struggled to pull out
of nowhere the stone at the bottom of a pool hiding since
earth came into being what was the moment that my eyes
did not know but makes them cry the way dust sometimes
invisible enters your eyes I was a girl who laughed at the
whims of passing faces the world came to an end when I fell
into deep sleep I wait for the unwaitable that life may
achieve blissfulness of death in life in one movie scenarios
change phenomenally fast I was thinking of the woman
who saw the girl at the doorstep it was her heart left behind
as one leaves her luggage in the waiting room of a railway
station did life really go by without acknowledging this
sadness of mine as sadness I sit in this room and the thought
comes to mind whether light occupies more space than my
eyes do I am a piece of nothingness who can feel pain and
believe that it is real I understood change when I was
touched by the rod of God with the idea of one God I
associated a standard language spoken by everyone in the

idea of many gods I saw local languages flourish but you were to me the languages that people used the jokes they made impromptu the minutes of their lives spent in talking to themselves about others the languages of others that gave meaning to minutes I pandered to ghosts that came into my bed through the open window of the kitchen when my eyes close you must be turning into a ghost the universe one afternoon opened the curtain for my searching soul all definitions boiled down to the distinction between homoeroticism and homosexuality life was as real as love when there was no interest attached to it the notion of life as an automaton was problematic because it closed the margins to the startling ironies of being with others I lived and there was nothing to achieve in my living but to blast the bubbles of misfortune that smiled on me like a lover bending to kiss the child I was a bubble and out of the bubble came the child murderers and stealers of hearts fell in the same category as the devil no goldsmith is to be seriously trusted yellow gold can be changed to white gold with silver and red gold with copper gold can change in the hands of the goldsmith my heart was red and white the goldsmith is the devil of a lover when it comes to changing the color of the heart the lover writes but the beloved is the agent of transformation the beloved is the goldsmith of hearts I give my trust as I laugh at changing colors I can accept separation only when I am convinced that we are inseparable as the hardness of a rock from the rock itself I do not want to make a move unless you move to throw the mask of being and let me know you that my inside is burning like the forehead of a child who refuses to get out of bed for fear the water does not go down her throat I concentrate on my stomach and not on my brain I defecate through my veins the feces of an intelligence that is sensitive to the rhythm of ducks in water circles never stand

still in a scenario where I am exhausted waiting for the last
circle to disperse into the serenity of a time before the flux
of light from perfumed candles filled the plains
with blue music of rain.

Cosmetics

I don't see you and I am upset for long. I see you and I am
upset that I won't be seeing you for long. Is it the act of
seeing an open window or the usage of language that
visualizes what happens behind closed windows this thing
between you and me is the sky castaway among seas of
humanity from a lover of stones I turned into a lover of
rivers and bodies the stones I never forgot they had scales
of a fish on them the lines were esoteric it could not have
been the hand of a man or a woman maybe a
hermaphrodite that wrote in undecodable codes the
naturalist has a way of improvising on nature of things and
believing that it is natural for bucket to float on water
before water lets it sink on dangerous terrains I was lost
among ironies of unrealizable expectations I relished the
opportunity to talk about future with no thought of
tomorrow the future was further away than the setting sun
now you were a mocking ray of hope that would never let
me go how could I show my pregnant body to you that are
my lover the lover epitomizes aesthetics unlike the husband
that is there in a physical space as angel of my heart black
ironic eyes looking beyond my dreams the thing that
distinguished the homoerotic from homosexual arched over
me like rainbow from horizon to horizon I was a
theoretician of bodies that indulged in all kinds of cosmetics
homoerotic is the light homosexual is the dark homoerotic
is my neighborhood homosexual is the state of being
pigeons are homoerotic doves are homosexual lions are
homosexual tigers are homoerotic I never disputed the
kindness of life a woman who saw in cosmetics another
reality of sun falling on red tiles of houses standing upon
hills from disconnected images I made necklaces that kept

breaking under weight of my neck but the weight of the necklace I felt more in the absence of the necklace my neck was touched by thought of a necklace waterless wells are my desires for beautiful moments I am unconventional in the way mothers tend to be when taking care of truant children you learn from experience that this truant child called living can only be loved not as a matter of choice but in the way we will things to happen with that zest for absent necklaces in the distant wells of deserts life had a way of cutting meanings short when I believed that a story could fit in anywhere merely with a change in names that was the essence of my cosmetics which had some kind of universal morality as its basis pregnancy gave me a dimension unexplored I came out of the mountain of sameness I felt the constant need to throw out the scream inside me is muffled but I can hear it in the sketch of a white flower on a white canvas the era of cosmetics has begun we arranged our lives in shadows we were born to die while the rest of the world lived in the corner where the bird waits plate on a plate is a rock the kiss of a star on my bed the dancers of the sky invite me to their heavenly abode a nerve on the left of my forehead is deeply disturbed and causes me to sprint along a path cosmetics is a reflection upon columns of light and dark in the cosmos tell that to my heart that you will not let me imagine dying in your arms I would die rather than be tortured your love of trinkets holds me in one piece I hear the sound of pieces falling and I am tortured in my cosmetic imagination I make jokes and laugh at the same with due respect my soul is tarnished with vices the idea of dying in a brothel is the favorite of my vices it is a reliving of adolescence when everything was made up seasons wander on this planet like holiday makers that keep returning year after year to the same place the memories have changed my pregnancy has

given me long hard nails I need to paint them with the color
of my eyes when you see my nails you will
not miss my eyes.

Incredible showrooms. We turned off lights and walked toward the kitchen. In doorways life began with little lamps spread out to denote a sense of festivity. I like being pregnant. My face turns serene despite what my body is going through. There is a glimmer of evening light in the eyes. Will I ever be the same again? My body changes with coming of the child. I put on weight that I will not lose. It is an instance of abstract art coming into being. I am depressed when I see my body change its contours. What is the road that goes to Damascus if I am a traveler standing on the Great Wall of China? The question is irrelevant to the fact that I have lived in one tiny village with few connections in the neighboring village for most of my life. Abstract were those jokes that we made on farms. I became an artist when I thought about the child that filled my space. I rendered what I felt in rhythms of a kind nobody understood. They were unique to my body. Pregnancy gave me a different sense of time. The world was made in roughly nine months. That was the world of my mother. My world took approximately the same time. It sprang as a bud from nowhere. Metaphors of sacrifice do not amuse me. I prefer pleasures of the body. I am pregnant with nothing when I am not pleased with my world. I am an abstract artist dealing in worlds. I come when I want to come and the world is a pond of flames with golden fish in it. We are twisted ironies of a twisted fate. It explains my fondness of the polemics of pregnancy. The poetry of objects is inscribed in gestures of my body. In erotic environments I'm meticulously attached to tacit words that come out of the feminine. I am misfit in my culture. I am misfit elsewhere too. Why should I become a hat when I can simply be a feather. I rarely forgot hurts I received in love. I forgot that I was angry with a person I gave myself to in the summer of the year 2139. I could be forgiving when the hurt was never there at all. Birds and happiness I choose and the rest I leave to circumstances. Children and sea tend to be abstract in my equally abstract eyes. My soul is brevity personified in a beam of moonlight. My body is the moon herself. Young I sought companionship. Younger I became with age. My spirit had the quality of a dynamo. No space gave me the sense of exile. When I thought I was going home it was only to touch the body of a friend. Pregnant I remembered the body more often for no other reason except that I had time to do so. Freedom is a word that has no meaning in poverty. I believed that I had chosen the ones I loved in the freedom of my expanding body. I called it patriotism when I loved friends. I discovered new words for each situation that I was placed in. What I always believed I needed and could not do without was the support of other women. Pregnancy convinced me of that. I was a chicken that crossed the street. It did not take much to do that. I had to keep my eyes watching my fluttering heart. Did I cross the road or was I imagining that I did. There was a tree on the other side of the road and now I stand in the shade of that tree. Does that mean that I am not hungry or I don't need shade for my body to relax. Doubts are for the distrustful. I trust my belly and its hunger for life. I made a living by cooking food and dreaming the impossible. From the sanity of mornings I normally relapsed into the insanities of night. What was life other than the pause that had in its womb the answer to unasked questions. Formalities are for the frivolous. I was formally invited to a dinner. Frivolously I accepted it. I cut wood before I cooked food. I dreamt the impossible that I swam in waters of paradise. Pregnancy gave edginess to my responses. I am

not earth to be trampled upon and my feelings are not on
sale. I am you when you are not conscious of
your self as self.

I go through phases unnatural as that which glitters as gold
but may not be gold. I have reason to believe that I see a
diadem of infinite blue around mouths of strangers. The
doors of the cage keep closing around me. In mouths of
strangers I discover freedom. In the mouth of passion I
destroyed the cage of reason. Stone I turn into when pushed
from the edge of a cliff. Falling I enter the body of a
vampire and read at nights. I have the vague apprehension
of an actor offstage that things are not meant to turn right. I
had to escape from words in order to be another person.
Was I a word constituted in space. I avoided the life of an
insect that filled me with shame of an unbearable kind. That
was not projection as much as being. Was I breaking a heart
with an axe long as the middle finger of my best enemy and
worst friend. I am not used to a quiet house where waves of
silence flow into my face. I am not watching sleepers who
are watched by their grave inner selves. My back is turned
toward them. I am watched by that which is silent and puts
its arms around my waist. My hands are in the hair of a
sleeper. That which loves me with no condition is entitled
to receive the touch of my finger. None but that which
loves to plant a kiss on my raised chin. What is it that loves
to bite my ears and throw my spirit into a state of
confusion. It is the mouth of a stranger in narrowest of
lanes that connects one broken bridge with another. The
bottles are open for tongues to delve into lost secrets of the
mouth. I threw a bottle into the mouth of a wave. Strange
the wave smiled with serenity of a breast-sucking child. I
am familiar to the strange. The mentality of those who live
on the sunny side of hills tempts me to debunk ideologies
that debunk debunking. I come from the cold and wet side

of hills. I am outside owing to a sheer sense of desperation. Indoors it was raining through walls. With my mouth I clung to every drop of rain in desperation of a true debunker. That was the way I was raised as a raisin-eater with a capacity to alter facts at leisure. What attracted me to strangers was their tendency to believe the unbelievable. I liked the story of the rabbit that was discarded from nine villages because it told the truth and the lamp of the leopard that burnt until dawn because it was a liar. I needed the arms of a friend to find my way into the world. Call me a romantic who kisses with her eyes open. In the middle of winter your voice is an instant of spring that revives the orchestra of the landscape. Momentous was the moment of revival. I was a landscapist who actualized impressions before I became an architect of passion who executed spaces. Houses were born when adobe came in contact with sun to make the language of my hand. Adobe, the sun and my hands. I was a masterpiece of an illusion even when they called me the dreamer of carnations. Pregnancy made me sleepy most of the time. As words, gelatin and wistful go together for me. Wistful meant moving toward the state of gelatin. Gelatin implied a relationship that had long turned sour and built on bygone sweetness. I was wistful for sweetness that turned stale. That was me and what could I say but whistle tunes of unspeakable kind that provoked the passersby to stone me to death. This was in the year 2139. I documented those moments as if they were in the future. All I cared to notice were the hands of the stone-thrower. From a distance I smelt adobe. Hot were those hands that touched stones. The imminence of dying with stones seemed more lustrous than living without ever calling fate to bed. Fate is the smarter of us two. With poisoned lips I kissed fate. Fate was prepared with an antidote to fatality. As an unreasonable poet I had to go

down on my knees for being a worshipper of stones. I
hugged the stone that took away the last ray of
light from my eyes.

Enclaved. If you ask me I can turn fire into water. If you do not ask me I can let water be water and fire remain fire. That's beside the point. I am enclaved in a room waiting for the knock at the door. Life is a street circus and I am a tightrope walker. I performed with a cry the day I was born. I was naked and dismally unaware of it. I suffer to wait without waiting to suffer. That is unfair to one I love. I don't need to see you because you already are there for me in mirrors without reflections. Will you venture into the world tonight before birds are ready to go to sleep? I absorbed sand with my soul and you came into mind. I want to believe what my body insists that my soul must believe. When I am hungry for love as if it were bread my soul is convinced that the need is real. I am enclaved in a circus with trained animals. Waiting I learnt to appreciate the colors of silence. I yearned not to wait thinking that yearning will let me forget the bitter music of unforgettable memories that echo through my body. The circus was coming to a close and the street was closing down on me. In a flash I realized how unimportant punctuation marks were. Teachers taught me that at school. The manners of an age are in the manner that beings lend their mouths to be kissed by another. I sighed to myself when I had no words left. Then I spoke endlessly until dawn broke down upon me. You don't realize that you are a person in me. You see the part that you see in the part that I am. Years it took me to explain myself to you. When you understood me in the part that I really was I was flying a kite some time late in the afternoon. I punished myself because my words would not hurt you. The body that made words had to be suitably disciplined. The body was hurt at my secret thoughts and it rose like a cornered animal in a dark room. I meditated on the harmony of discordant strings. I felt the juice of a mango in my mouth. I heard my body protest its innocence in the court of law while my soul loitered freely towards the market on a borrowed bicycle. At the turning point between court and market I saw the street circus in motion. I could not have seen light if your passion did not ignite electricity in the air. Electrocuted I changed forms. Darkness was without an agenda. I encroached on 'no trespassing' zones and let dogs catch the scent of my body. Dogginess was my nature. The dogs merely caught the scent of another one like them in all but form. Night is time for the dying and passionate. In the hope of finding a trace of blood the mosquito turned into mercenary. With might of my soul I opposed the aspirations of the mosquito. The darkness complicated a dark situation. I am a mere onlooker of a street circus. There is no reason to believe that I am the warrior who can encounter the mosquito. The circus was my life and I chose the street for the occasion of displaying my tendency to be a passive love-maker. I succeeded in getting out of the enclave but I returned long before it was too late. The nest knew the bird better than the bird knew the nest. I never took the returning seriously as much as spending of the day in beds that were flat enough to hold my sprained back. The hardness of bed functioned as a massage for the back. I was fresh and the lightness of morning was lemon to my tongue. The sourness had the effect of taking me on holidays where I lived with circus performers of the street. In sunlight the river had the look of milk and water tasted of honey. The flower of a pomegranate knocked at my door. I was content as sparrows in background. Our life that insisted upon its reality was a wall painting with a woman's face that looked at you from every possible angle. I was a child and the street circus was the essence of my childhood.

Time was not an issue for the passionate kisser. She turned
up at the oddest times of the day. Lovely as amber beads
were those kisses. The moral question involves the will and
hence is a question of passion. I stand at the door of your
house. I could walk away as if nothing happened. I waited
and turned the bond of attachment to one of love. The night
offered plenty of opportunities for one impaled by passion.

How much you mean to me you will never know. I
surprise myself with my great unknowing. It is unknowing
concealed in tears on a blade of grass. Imagination is mother
of reason. How could I have a reason without an image to
support its existence. It must be the way I was raised to
think about pomegranates. All fruits taste funny when
compared to the lover's mouth. I chose to be the beloved
that celebrated herself. You were the sort of lover who sort
of dealt with pomegranates as what the mouth sort of
naturally savored. My world is at peace when flowers
merge with fantasies. I am perfectly docile when it comes to
body movements of exiles who call themselves exiles.
Exiles are preoccupied with nothing. I am bound by words
in the rain which fail the test of commitment in sunlight. If
the heart reasoned then the mind went as far as to imagine
hill slopes with tea plants greening the air. I am suspicious
of dictionaries that attribute meanings to words. Meanings
are divided along lines of fashion. Just now it is fashionable
for kisses to be compared to amber beads. The fashion
changes with change in meaning. The fashion changes
meaning as well. Nothing would be more to the point than
to publish books without names of authors. Unfulfilled
obligations drove me from city to city. For some time it was
the amusement of anonymity. Once I sensed familiarity

returning like the smell of chimney I had to leave. That's how I discovered the meaning of decadence. It was not in fashion then. It did not change either as far as my life is concerned. Once I wore the mask of the giver it looked like the world needed me more than I needed the world. To the quiet river it made no difference whether there were swimmers in it or not. I took from trees a sense of awareness of distances but I lived in a sensuality that resembled birds. My return to what I believed was familiar made me realize the strangeness of things. If a rose and a letter are on the same table I want to be able to comprehend the connections between two different discourses. Juxtaposition is nonsense. It cannot be the basis of a poem. That would be turning fashion into a fashion for fashion's sake. The bird in my bed was the projection of a space external to reason. I could still imagine it. I am so confused that I don't know what it is that confuses me. I take away your breath when I talk about love. I am confused by your resistance to my words. I can stop talking at the peril of a pearl losing its luster. I keep amber beads in my pocket as a charm to drive away the madness of the perpetual exile in me. I feel the loveliness of belonging to early summer breeze. The happiness of death is not in flowers that circle my body. It is loveliness of amber beads that carried me through life. Self-referentiality constituted my style of writing without the self in any way referring to me. The I that I speak about is me for all purposes that are ideal and not real. In reality I share the presence of amber beads though I cannot claim the same degree of loveliness or love. Sad and foolish are essential traits of my real person. Ideally I am smart as a wild goat that has escaped the gaze of hunter. I am an amber bead of my existence. I hide selves within pockets of my self. I use my own self as a charm against myself. I could be lovely in a self that is not a self

and a memory that cannot bring out any recollections
to an absent self.

For myself I cannot claim the same innocence that I claim for my love. I affect you with words but you affect me without a word. Not a look or a gesture. Woman, my innermost body, what is the message I receive that you have not uttered with lips or hair. I may be passive. Active I might have killed you. Pregnant I am overwhelmed with a new sense of activity. In my hands you die the sensual death of sun dissolving in night. At thirty-three Christ completed his mission of empowering the most afflicted sections of humanity. At thirty-four I waited for my lover to arrive before night made way for dawn. I spoke about a faithless generation when I spoke about forced identification of prayer with religion. Infidels populated institutions and lovers stood outside in rain lips locked around lips. When love became isolated from infidelity it turned into something less than ordinary. From an infidel I evolved into a lover. Was my love a sweet mask for unsophisticated infidelity? The way faces of cities refuse to acknowledge that they were originally villages. Issues issued from forms reformed. The issue of infidelity versus love rose with formation of a culture that privileged roses to thorns. If the thorn were proof of my love the rose could be essence of my infidelity. The space of life is a boat stuck in sands of a beach. Better that way I felt for an essentially non-swimmer. The water was all mine because it filled the extent of my sight. Issues were formed overnight where lovers battled with infidels for voices of night articulate as the sea. I am bilingual to the extent that I understand languages of sea and night. On a night standing beside the sea I decided to move. I had to satisfy my innate curiosity to know clouds in other parts of earth. Did they wander as melodiously with same rhythm as above the ground that I stood. If I put my soul into your soul I could be a writer of ghazals. I drew an arrow from a rusted quiver and shot it into a tree. The tree wept and the arrow suffered. A friendship is brought to test. What constitutes the erotic is a thought of the body. In the negation of thought the sacred emerges as a repertoire of images. Christ is right in recognizing the intrinsic danger of thoughts. His boundless compassion is reserved for images like the blind person and prostitute. It brought out his deep fondness of the visual. The thought becomes an image for society to coexist with a notion of moral responsibility. Passion is intellectual and cannot be conceived without morality. Societies are amoral in the extreme sense that we observe in mobs and in the way majorities perceive minorities. Moral passion is generated among intellectuals who come out of oppressed classes. Their language is real because it connects to life. Christ borrows his language from those classes. He repays the debt of what he took from the poor with death on the cross. His death was an image and not a thought. It is hard to know why Christ took thoughts so seriously. A possible explanation is that his pity for the oppressed made him feel that thoughts had to be controlled. Thoughts were possessions that meant power over powerless. Lust is thought while love is imagined. Christ the matador takes the bull of thoughts by horns wresting it out of the ring of servitude. His rejection of thought is a rejection of patriarchy despite being the father's only child who will die to free the father of his sense of possession. The sacred was an alternative because artists had to be with minorities. Does that mean the sacred will disappear when there are no hierarchies and lovers will at last be reconciled with infidels? It is the existing division between thought and image that is the basis of class society. The thought will coexist with image in the body of the sacred where possession is not an issue any longer. I thought of you as lover. You turned out to be an infidel who transgressed rules as if it were the image that love was made of.

If eternity had eyes the dust of things would blind it. I let mosquitoes draw a bit of blood through pores of my skin. That would enhance my claims to martyrdom. Titillation is bad for the superstitious. Black cats on quiet roads titillate me to rewrite my life with blood taken from the mosquito's body. Centrality lost its meaning for me when I had to part from a friend. The center I denied to words I could not when it came to your eyes. That is what your eyes did to me. I lost my center while they steadily looked into my soul. You know my words that move more than I know your eyes that stare straight into eternity. I write or I die and I choose to write. I discount all possibilities of life except the poetic. Infinite love is incompatible with hell or that love is not infinite. In the end love has to be good enough to absorb evil. If the universe is creation of one God then it is he who is in conflict. He must be convinced that mercy is greater than justice. Not me. I am angry at the way you take my feelings for granted. If God is beyond contradictions then it is not possible that he manifests himself in contradictions. If the contradictions do not belong to him how do I know him as God. What are the attributes in creation that are without contradictions. When it rains it does not stop raining on the houses of the poor who live in slums. Miserably hot summers take a toll on daily wage laborers. Armies and bureaucracies are not guided by the principle of compassion. Men use a language that men know and understand in the very idea of attributing manhood to God. The attributes of God cannot exist without contradictions. If God is neither love nor mercy because he is without opposition then he is nothing. I am nothing but a nothing in you. I waited for you as if you were eternity itself. I waited for you eternally and when you left it was as if you had never been with me. Your eyes make me believe that God is the noblest of all possibilities in human languages. I must be forgiven for using the narrow word human to speak about a narrower word language or God. Possibilities exist everywhere. That doesn't mean that you understand me in the same breath that I understand you. I wait for knowledge to happen and all I am given are possibilities. The knowledge that will take away the need in me to wait for you. I don't want to cry because pregnant I am afraid to produce a sad child. I am a sad child happy with every possibility except the one that takes you away from me. Age is a metaphor of forgetting. Early in life I went back to the past. It was early but I waited to see the mask of death. Poets claim that it is black. I have a feeling it is colorless. Nothing I wait for nothing. How can I know colorlessness in the same way that I cannot know nothingness? If I knew nothingness there is an excellent possibility to say that I do not know. Now I see quiet roads. Now I don't see black cats. Which one of them is really there is the question. The king of fools throws a blanket on fires. Weaker I am getting with each passing day. My eyes smile for cigarettes and the heart cries from craving a moment of peace. I am talking like a child. June is the time of movement from mimesis to mimicry. From an intellectual I become a joker. As a king I learnt to play the fool rather than represent one. Fire was a problem in hearts of the neighborhood. I threw a blanket before I turned to ash. That was my last act of folly. From then on life was a joke to me. Death had to come from the backdoor of my house because dogs of the street hung around during nights. These dogs hardly slept with their immense need for excitement. When I returned home in early hours from a friend I looked for black cats. The roads were quieter than

steps of black cats. The cats stood out as if they were
epitomes of eternities. Black roads trembled
at quiet footsteps.

Vulnerability of Grass

If love had a face it would be you lying on a bench in a garden and marking the number of leaves on ground with your eyes. Does that mean death is inevitable for the face of love to be dismantled by stupor of fallen leaves. Would that face be love if it did not share the sorrow of fallen leaves. In my veins I shared the vulnerability of grass. That was my rebellion against the world of feet that stepped on me. Vulnerable as grass I sustained the sun and encountered the storm. I lived for no other reason except that grass is yellow when it is not green. My politics is who I am. I am a garden lizard on a wall and a whiff of childhood enters my blood stream. The earth is covered with wet grass and I am a pair of eyes on other side of a dewy windowpane. In the time before the world made its appearance life was inseparable from death. Born I knew pangs of separation that tore into my flesh and made me eat my guts out. I am a gut-eater of a writer. I made myths where soul perspired in heat of body in states of oneness. I dissociated my tired soul from burning skin. Passion exhausted soul while skin sought to be touched by water. Magicians appeal to me less than matchsticks. The metaphysics of the line that makes sense is in fire of spaces and not magic of words. Words are occupiers of space. Masters they may seem for the time being but they exist because of spaces. My stomach is bloating. It could be the baby growing in me. I am hungry and tired most of the time. I am anxious of the body's changing contours. I like to indulge in preoccupations as if they were real. I recognize the reality of women from poverty vulnerable to hands of men who think and feel like men. They are not preoccupied with gaining weight. They are trying to survive. Vulnerability is a social condition. I am vulnerable to sufferings of all things. I translate my isolation into a discourse of resistance. The child in me will understand that she belongs to the present. The present must change in order for future to be different. Bread without freedom is inconceivable drudgery. Freedom without bread is a lie. When contradictions are naturalized they turn into paradoxes. Paradoxes are vulnerable to light of day. Myths are paradoxes just as paradoxes are myths of logical unresolvability. Poetry is the genre that recognizes the power of paradox. The paradox of the monkey in moon illustrates that there are no monkeys in the moon. That is not sufficient reason for us not to talk about the monkey in moon. The material condition speaks to us as life. It makes me wary of the fact that I am vulnerable as china when it is not green as grass. China are my eyes and china is my heart. I respect the reality of the sufferer though I can't deny that it implies the translation of a discourse. I loved you without ever living up to your expectations in me. I failed your trust and loved you all the more. I punished my soul for agony that my body had put you through. I denied my soul the joy of your company. When sleep took over me I was awake struggling minute through minute the loneliness of a lover who betrays but never smiles. I looked at nineteen houses on nineteen different streets before I lived in the house on the corner. Solicitation is a way of talking about fate without using figures. I solicited shadows on walls of a harem. No one lived behind these walls except grass that was vulnerable to caresses of the wind. Unlike windows walls provoked my attention to things I could never know. One of them was your heart. It had a window but walls of your eyes prevented me from peering into unknown. The walls of eyes preserved the window of the heart. Estranged from what I knew and a stranger to what I could never know I lay my head on grass and let stars overwhelm my impenetrable being.

In a changed context certain words mean nothing. If the mind of the person overlaps with language of mind then the difference between ethereal and esoteric is nominal. The secret of life is in air. I sense spring in the neighborhood. It is air that rouses secrets of my sleeping soul. I nurture a being in my belly. I need to drink milk though I hate it. Things seem to lose their taste with me for no reason and I continue to make love with the notion in head that there were beginnings without endings. That was how new love started between the persona and flower. It was love that saw no other alternative but to love. The persona envied the bee because it drew the essence of flower from what essentially did not belong to the flower. The contours of persona could be seen in fragrance of flower. The flower did not like being touched by persona. For the persona the essence of flower was in fragrance that came from some underground terrain of the flower's being. The bee dared to draw essence from the well of fragrances. The persona dreaded loss of fragrance. The flower recoiled at the touch of persona. The flower attempted to communicate to persona that the bee was related to function of its being.

The persona moved closer to flower in the hope of reconciliation. The flower resisted the touch of persona with same innocence that persona envied the bee. The well of fragrances was boundless as a water cloud. Logic came from emptiness. The world was real following a bout of emptiness. Eternity was possible in a fraction of space. Reality was in fragrance of the flower. The persona suffered to be annihilated by fragrance. It stirred shades of persona to very depths of non-being. The non-being rose into thin air. The seeds of time in matter and the historic

accident of emergence of consciousness that learnt that
separation was an art that could be accomplished with a
smile or a tear the thinning lip or the thickening tear wet
smile and dry tear the glance that smiles while tearing into
vacuum the gushing tear out of the smile of a hungry lip the
persona that flowers with fragrance of salty tears the flower
that smiles at attempts of the persona to impersonate the
flower a flower is a persona of the idea of flower that is a
persona of fragrance in the nostrils of a persona that loves
the idea of being in love with flowers as personas all ideas
are personas but not all personas are ideas what happened to
eye that spoke about the I as if the I was the eye of persona
the I of persona is a flower and the eye of the flower is the
aura that surrounds deathless dawns this intense quiet that
accommodates the breath of lovers this blackness that looks
like the hall of a sleeping god that can be watched at that
time when matter is resolved not to change time is
contained in mind of matter the heart of matter is in space
of fragrance that is non-space it occupies no volume it is
weightless it cannot be seen my heart is flooded with
fragrance thoughts rush in direction of wind that is scented
with light from shadows the nail in the finger that is
attachment of the persona to flower cast away in delirium of
splitting rhythms fragrance burst upon fires of cremation
the ground is hallowed with coming of ash the fragrance of
ash belongs to the moment but the moment has passed a
crow sits with a bone alone examining with scientific
precision the contents of bone the fragrance of bone in
memories of the living the misgivings of an unforgettable
past go down the river where ashes are dispersed what is a
word without intonation what is intonation without the eye
that pronounces the stage for the word to enter what
is it that is pronounced but no one
has heard of.

Amnesia of Late Youth

In the end. What was that? I hear mice squealing in background. Lovelessness is life and the world goes around on its own feet. I bought the daring presumption that there was life before me and after me. In those days I had a young and narrow face and my eyes were sad. My face continues to be narrow but my eyes don't seem sad anymore. Age has weakened my tendency to dramatize. I wet myself with curiosity thinking of burning leaves. You are my friend because I weep for you. It could be you who makes me cry. My small self is my childhood walking through doors of a house that smelt of my mother's bosom. Pregnancy maximized my sense of smell and I kept entering the past from the backdoor of future. In one go you say two things. It is day and night. The fringe is not a ring. The corners of the universe are lost in infinity. I understand you leave the throne of reason and enter the carpet of imagination. My head is a circle for dogs and my heart is a trajectory for horses. The world fell apart when I went to a city without a garden. I welcomed the falling apart of city because that was a phase of my life that I associated with sex. Words were my sexuality driven from straits of the city to the core of being. A bed is not for sleeping. I wrote my life in a bed about a series of beds that my body had constructed without purpose. My body never got used to beds in a hotel. They were merely for sleeping. The beds of thorns stayed in my soul longer than beds of roses. That was life. On a devil of a bed I lay one evening thinking of other beds that I had carefully forgotten. I was nervous and afraid. The thorn battled with rose and the scars of battle caused amnesia in my soul. My late youth was bliss of the drugged patient on a hospital bed. Black and yellow and white. The lamp on the tree besides. Anklets wild and picturesque strung with gems of distortion. They distorted stars of night. When the dancer is on her feet the universe is moving. States of matter profiled in a camera hidden in the chest. Touch my bed with your breath and I can prove that I love you with my soul. The phrase–things pass–has no meaning for me beyond the fact that things pass. Passing things caused a crisis in belly. I had a stomachache that looked like birth pangs. I missed the shore when the boat was far at sea. I jumped off the boat when I saw birds and the silhouette of trees in the mist of dawn. Was the shore waiting for me while I moved from place to place in the hope of finding succor for my failing stomach. The friends on boat confirmed to me that the shore waited for no one. It was just there like a blob of matter unconscious and self-contained. I sought the shore just as if the sea had no meaning if somewhere it did not touch land. The shore meant a sort of critical departure of my self from myself. The meaning of struggle was in struggle. The rest was a dream that stood like a lampshade on a lamp braving the storm. The unthinkable was the irresolvable because it was disconnected from all thoughts of shore. Stories are discourses of fantasies. They espouse nothing. I fantasize about shores with pleasure when I read a story. The fantasy cannot help reaching out to life. Amnesiac in my late youth the fantasies kept coming back but it was life in them that elated me beyond the confines of words. Words are prisons. The amnesiac returned to the same prison and each time the prison had newness of fresh paint on it. The shapes of dilapidated walls were never the same. They recurred as fantastic lives in the soul of the amnesiac. Philosophy is vain and psychology does not exist because the fantastic cannot analyze the fantastic. Between bushes and corridors I choose neither. I devoted my life to remembering pieces of a mirror. In the end I was a child of cafes and kitchens. My stories of life came from the smell of food and the dust of streets.

The Bird that Never Returns

Glossing over presuppositions. The cause is connected to cause and effect to effect. But both are not connected to each other. I felt the happiness of light touched by spirit of silence when the vista of eyes grasped a moving speck that resembled flowers of paradise. What happens to the bird that never returns. I question the physicality of memory. If it cannot be held in my hands will memory turn blue with biliousness. It points to the fact that there was never a memory of an approaching speck in wind that had the semblance of paradise. The world has already come to an end in the past. What is to come has no end in view. Why must the bird return if light claims to be inseparable from the world of shadows. The bird will not change the flight of shadows from the lightness of things. Happiness made me sing the song in the memory of my soul. My soul was innocent of any conception of a life after life. It remembered but it could not foretell. The dreams of soul were composed of materials taken from earth that could make a house. Structures are fallible but dreams are not. My soul was naught. In the naughtness of soul dreams infallibly encountered reality as material structures would resist rain.

The rain trickles in my soul. What are these afternoons when I want to sleep and the bird of my dreams manifests itself as sun revealing in drops of rain the poetry of colors. My soul is a dreamer and not an idealist. I want to spread my hands and fly from the top of the tallest mountain. That is the only way I can translate ideas into dreams. The bird can never fall because it is saved by flights of fantasy. How can I miss or be missed when I am in a fantasy. My flight dispenses with memories. I fly and memory is a ghost that arrives before and waits to receive me with arms wide open.

I keep a fantastic distance between the host and me. My self knows itself as myself. From two words we turn into one and imagine that it makes a difference. In one word I am not divided. With a united self I refuse to surrender my soul to reality. My dreams are armed to teeth with roses strewn on paths of reality. I am invisible to dreamless eyes. Poor reality. I railed against it more than anything else. Create the space for an exploration campaign. I am due to dwell in dreams for the next few moments or years of my life. In dreams I struggled with dreams. I was a realty dealer. I sold realities and bought dreams with the same money. I pawned those dreams in the bazaar of borrowers and became a houri for the love of saved souls. A houri I am and may I be forgiven if I failed souls who denied the world for joys of paradise I have a fate without fortune because it denies me things I want I measure my fortune with the number of dew drops on petals of a jasmine flower I said what I felt and I felt when I had nothing to say but look with the infinity of children or animals natural in that thoughtless way my life composed of all these dead moments the beginning no different from the end the turn of events entirely eventless when it came to the bubble that burst on the face of the unfamiliar the strange is not what makes the stranger objects are constituted in perceptions the stranger is the perception and not the object because there is no object lying there it has already passed into gloom do I see the bird in future or is it in my perception of the same I wander along with my gaze attempting to follow the course of the bird there was no course and the bird was a dot of blackness on an orange sky I am identified by folks as a character in a folktale nothing is supposed to return the idea of return is a presupposition I glossed over with my spectacles falling on the ground.

Mountains Crumble When the Earth Quakes

The truth is bitter but bitterer than truth is the lie that looks like truth. Precious is time that illuminates the passion of the book words breaking through the hands into my pen the letters are in red and black I would wait for death to arrive with the mystery of a stranger's mouth close to mine my tongue is full of lies or half-truths as I call them my life functions in phases but none of them can out beat the phase when I started aging with the impulsiveness of a brooding pensioner with unproductive longings of the future alone in the universe I thought of God as a roommate at home I never felt at home in exotic surroundings I was ordinary homesickness is for those who are sick of home I was loved by men who confused me for a swan it was my commitment to a politics of irresolution that meant certainty in no terms but the most uncertain ones my inability to engineer any serious emotion because of my stomach that hurt while I talked the cramps that came out of stress I had to use the mountain route that curved in inexplicable ways at the moment there is no alternative to our relationship being sour as vinegar I miss the food and the hands on my cheeks my face moving toward the breasts of my loved one like salt in water the thrill of being pregnant is the consciousness of another blossoming in the self-same body seven moments of ecstasy I counted them if not for seven it would've been nine but it stopped at seven odd numbers touch my body that pringles at the sound of seven or nine seven times I missed the dawn nine times I thought of waking up before the sun hit the ground I kept my suffering a secret because seven colors of day could not accommodate nine moods of night seven times seven the earth had mercy on my madness nine times nine I was

madder than ever and had no inkling of what the earth
meant by showing mercy to the lover of windows in the
seventh hour I had a premonition that I would see the girl
of my seventh year on the seventh night of the seventh day
in the seventh dream of the seventh hour in the ninth hour
and the ninth dream I saw the girl in the ninth phase of the
moon seven and nine together did not coincide with six and
seven which is the year I was born and Israel invaded and
occupied Palestinian territories my loves are in sevens my
passions are in nines I heard seven notes and my soul took a
sevener high in the seven mountains nine melodies crept
down my spine I tingled with delight seven times I changed
my world for seven pistachios nine times I gave my soul for
nine kisses supernatural is seven and sweet is nine my soul
dropped seven tears when it touched the seventh word of
the seventh ghazal of Hafiz nine lives I was destined to live
and in the ninth life I saw nine needles standing on their
heads and walking toward the ninth bier that had the coffin
of the ninth most loved saint since the beginning of history
called the eunuch that spent its ninth life revolving in nines
seven times I was disappointed in love nine times I was a
lover of bodies who showed no sign of withdrawing from
the field of the battle seven times earth went around the sun
nine times bees sucked the nectar out of lips of flowers
seven is king of hearts nine is queen of spades seven times I
notice your feet make seven steps toward the ocean nine
times I kiss your hands in blind love seven was a symbol of
the order nine was chaos beneath order at seven I finished
the chores of day at nine I began the night of wine and
wistfulness seven days cannot imagine the idea of nine
nights but nine nights can easily conceive seven days in
their wombs where days lie in cool shade on seven walls of
an imaginary castle I saw nine blades of grass painted on
each wall seven times I was angry with you nine times I

forgave myself seven is infinity but nine is nothingness
seven times mountains crumbled and nine times
the earth quaked.

An unrecognized actor is an actor of a kind. What makes realism different from reality that supposedly stood outside all discourses. Just as realism has nothing to do with reality, reality has nothing to do with something being or not being there. Realism reduces reality to itself. Reality reduces itself to being there. If reality was not there in the form of a beetroot that has a taste that is so beetrootish and that color a weird mixture of blue and red and violet and purple you never see anywhere else but on the body of a beetroot then the realist has a point that something has to be there for it to be what it is what is not there is not necessarily invisible but something carefully concealed from one who contributes to making of life the happiness of labor is in the outcome the sharing of the fruit realism pretends that labor is secondary to organization that people are used to being ordered around and that that's the easiest way to make things happen and history is all about that while reality insists that there is something called nature that is there whether I am in this world or not that this nature is more natural than history because it has a being outside history I refute both claims without attempting to say anything profoundly new the unrecognized actor did not see the stage as stage but as life that was when the stage was life the stage did not have to occupy a place at odds with life with the artist being different from the worker the stage was not elevated above the ground once the stage left the ground the actor was recognized as actor the age of recognition gave rise to a new way of looking at the stage men called it history the others called it oppression the actors learnt that there was this thing called audience isolated from its own acting self the stage needed props to hold it and with its acting self appropriated the audience were dazzled with brilliance of another life so far away from the struggle of beings realism is a form of trading with concepts about reality history is a form of realism the reality is the past but it is not something there for my senses to inhale my bridges are burnt and my home is in turmoil what is my reality but wings of a dove that cannot fly the gaze of the dove sears the scorching sun the sun melts in agony of the dove's eye the ugliness of a real world is in separation of realism from reality and both from processes of struggles that constitute life the lives of owning classes lost their contact with life I was a dove in reality lying close to a ventilator in the backroom of the stage I had a bird's view of stage it suited the genetic complexities of my physiology to stay far away from the stage and within the stage a viewer but neither an audience nor an actor I took the view that shitting and pissing placed certain metaphysical constraints on people that came out as the need to understand each other the soul emerged from asshole and the heart from pisshole our wholeness was lost in parts life would be a lot simple if we did not have the psychological distance from our own shit and piss the very fact that the caste system thrives on purity versus pollution principle with the lower castes considered polluted has something to do with alienation from shit and piss there is no doubt that caste and class walked hand in hand with historic variations just as racism can to a large extent be interpreted from a class perspective the origins of realism are in oppression of the poor that is the reality concealed by realists who talk about shit and piss in an extraordinarily sanitized environment without daring to come anywhere near objects of their analysis because to them that's not the point how can I understand the past without delving into history and how can I accept this history as mine which talks about oppression in the most objective of terms.

Melodies for Moonstruck

A touch of aesthetics is good for the soul blistering in
the eye of the world. Complacency is bound to
meaninglessness. Life humbles us all whether we choose it
or not. There is a song for every moment that I am not
reeling in the prison of life. Every moment is a song in the
life of eternity when my mouth is pressed to windowpanes
and showers beat against lips without touching them. Fate is
the glass that separates lips from rain. How lips long to be
touched. How rain suffers the loss of lips. I came to the last
point when the word touches another word. There are no
words left in the basket of discourse. I forsook what I loved
when motherhood took a toll on my desiring body. Poems
of guilt cloaked in shame became a theme of my art. Life
has no meaning because the universe is not conscious of
itself as living but kindness does have a meaning or the
universe would not let men perpetrate their anger and lust
on those who wait for the hearts of their oppressors to
change. I was born and I waited for death to happen. I was
unborn and in a deathless state. Details impinge upon my
sensitivity as rays of sun on running waters. I absorb and I
reflect. The details of my life are devils of deception. I see
the bottom of a pool. I descend and my feet are far from the
bottom. I descend into your soul. There is no bottom. I am
deceived. Did I deceive myself or was it my eyes that saw
things wrong. I am color blind by default when it comes to
colors of another soul. If this abstract thing called life is
cruel does that justify my cruelty to others. I have no
dilemmas except the future and the future is not a dilemma
but the forehead of a girl I used to know back in time I
planted kisses on that forehead in the hope that they would
grow into little touch-me-nots that sleep when they are

touched and wake up when the seeming threat of unseeming touch is far away I keep a distance from the palate of the kisser because lips fold when I touch them and open when eyes disclose the purity of a child they bask in white tenderness the woman of flowers and the woman of fragrances shared the lifestyle of a parachute nostalgia is unbecoming for self-imposed exiles because what was never present is mourned as absence I could never repeat words and mean the same thing the words were new and the meanings were newer than the glaze of words echoed in the intonation of the speaker that is life's tragedy that culture teaches us to subscribe to meanings but life tells us that there are none culture comes into conflict with life and we stand helpless before the well-springs of our tragedy forced to take joy in what hurts us most I make melodies for the moonstruck that is when I have nothing better to do than watch fish in waters of a polluted lake I figure out that fish do not exactly have a long life but fish never think about life though scientific evidence points out that life began with the unicellular organisms known as prokaryotes if there are no universal discourses then the question of life is secondary to living stars burn with a casualness that is almost callous while fish subsist in infected waters the longest standing battle since history is that between sun god and moon-goddesses every other battle pales in comparison in terms of scope family sagas and swords thrust in soil of vineyards famines and the origins of fate betrayals of night and judgments of day laws and their dissociation from law-givers brothels and downtowns of mad cities the bananas of republics that lay claims to divine essences I like to be under the moon struck with love for a melody that opens the gates for the houris to leave paradise and descend to the bed of an oyster where the pearl of future is let out into sea of presences I feel the kindness of a gentle eye that smiles as it uncovers patterns on my discolored soul.

Midnight Lambs

The waves of the sea hit the wall of the house. The cruelty
of blue sky in the minds of men. The sun did not stop
shining throughout history. The nights were cool as ever.
The seasons did not have a problem with their cycles. It was
spring when it was spring and winter when it was winter.
Nature went on and so did the cruelty of men against
others. Change unsettled tradition and tradition rose with
vehemence to avenge the loss of authority. Men displaced
men while earth revolved on its own axis. I sat on shores of
life and counted waves of the sea. The real number was one
more than what I thought. I dream of figurines of clay and I
see you in the background of a frameless mirror. The writer
who dreamt of counting the number of waves passing
before her eyes in less than a moment did not detract from
voices of the past rolling in the back of her mind. Real
numbers make me insecure. I am unresolved though never
unhappy. Since I knew that there was life outside me I was
never unhappy for a day or a moment. I owe my
irresolution to metaphysics but my love of life comes from
the breath of one whose lips are on my ear. I have a hot
peppered tongue and she a cold wintry mouth. The
midnight lambs moved down slopes to enter the fortress of
black clouds guarded by thunder. It was lightning that
showed the way. Midnights made me soft as lamb. The
fortress of reason and with you I entered the precincts of
reason as midnight lambs sheared of all wistfulness and
ready to battle unreasonable walls that cannot be imagined
turned the world into offenders and defenders the walls
continued as if they had a life independent of the wills of
men and women I nailed a coffin to the wall for mere
aesthetics the wall responded with comic indifference that

was so like walls at nights I was chased by walls I left the
fortress and walked into the midnight of madness with you
I returned empowered as a ghost that can touch but not be
touched the spirit reigned supreme and lambs were ready to
be axed that reason's ramparts are filled with blood of lambs
on reddening ramparts the anarchists who were wedded to
passion came into being the world we turned upside down
the world turned us inside and out that's how passion met
the world and the world understood passion midnight lambs
in black and white midnight lambs in colors of twilight if
not for lambs what is the meaning of midnights and but for
midnights the lambs would be at loss of the flickering light
that hurls them towards the altar nothing takes the form of
the poetic apprehension of reality the poetic flounders
towards nothing the lamb is the least poetic of animals
because it is entrenched in symbolism like the rose that is
overdone as a symbol the dressing down of the lamb and
rose happens with changing frames the midnight being the
most visible of frames to the naked eye without an inkling
of light the lamb of my childhood inspired in me tears that
even onions could not the wounds of my soul can be healed
with kisses on my body I am a dealer in the dark I deal with
the dark the darkness is what I give to those who can see
perception is disastrous where the perceiver is drawn to
symbols the midnight is real without any symbol remotely
connected to it history succumbs to temptations of midnight
roads are symbols because they intrude upon reality of the
jungle my understanding of trees comes from walking along
roads but roads themselves are platitudes they stretch the
imagination to where the eye can see mirages upon mirages
rising I come from a small village far from the road about
two miles away and a variety of lives the women are
infinitely real and hardly symbolic when midnights arrive
they sport danger with the intelligence of lambs their

worlds take on other shapes so different from the world that we observe in geography textbooks.

The Kitchen and the Garden

I am a bubble dancing on shoreless waters. The mildest of fires is spent in morning hours gazing at receding pink of skies. There was never a sane person who crossed a mountain without remembering the sea. Who ever looked at stars and forgot the passing of time. In the semi-darkness of villages at dawn life began. The only real time is that of the farmer. You did not have to be a dreamer to know that separation of the kitchen from rest of the house leads to two major effects on culture. One was the association of women with making of food. The other was story-telling that began with the tongues of women just as song and dance was the outcome of laboring peasants who looked for rejuvenation and strength. Among nomads culture was not preserved as a set of habits isolated from subsistence but rather culture directly reflected the demands of subsistence. The gypsies are the romanticized and in effect feared, persecuted and avoided people who fall under this discourse. If stories began in kitchens poetry continued to be preoccupied with gardens of imagination. They were not words what mouth said to mouth. The communion of mouths carried in it the wholeness of being. It mattered to life that it must preserve itself for no reason other than that you turn the dust of summer into the bitter pill of friendship brought to test. The garden adjacent to kitchen sent vibes across my heart. Summer's dust stayed on leaves like a thin layer of brown varnish. From the center of kitchen I looked at flowers in the garden locked in a knot with the dust of daydreams. We sat on the ground and tasted food with our fingers that had this smell of spices. I never believed in belongings. When I went out of a place I carried the place as a set of picture-perfect images. I say that with irony implicit in the texture of images. The place was mine in essence but the belongings were the property of birds. I practically existed on the kitchen side of things and the smell of food began to induce sleep in me when it was not yet time. On the garden side of things I had to work for aesthetics to be sustained as aesthetics. Pictures are not perfect and neither are stories that men and women make up in the course of making the grain palatable. With Marx I attribute everything beautiful that life has to offer to struggle. The struggle was evident in stories of those who suffered for no reason and were aware of it. They knew the story of sunlight in the kitchen and thieves in the garden. One of the thieves was a lover out to meet the beloved of the kitchen. While the food was in the making love was performed with the hotness of wild steam filling the earth and heaven. Take the person as a picture of a unit of time. The times of peasant and the gypsy and women in and out of kitchens occupy the most space of life in the past. If the wall is white I could let it be white or raise questions about its whiteness. In kitchens gossip was the food of imagination. Kitchens of love and gardens of perfection. White walls made us ask names of workers who raised the walls. There were walls in stories of kitchens. The gardens were protected from eyes of the unexpected. The world was without walls. Wall-less worlds frightened me out of my wits. Life did not dare to forgive me because I never forgave it either for bringing me into this world. I was not asked if I loved the sky under which I am supposed to live my unit of time. The waters ejected me from the womb. I was nothing and I was not asked if I wanted to be something. I am something that knows that it is nothing. I am fire and salt. I am ritual of the morning with which light opens the curtains of day. I am the closing of eyes when desire puts the body to sleep. I am the kitchen that made life possible and the garden that the eye feasted upon.

I see echoes of others in what I write. Madness found me hiding behind a cupboard like children do in the game of hide and seek. Madness sought me for her child. I lived in madness as a matter of fact. There are biographies no autobiographies. One can never write about oneself as self. If I attempted an autobiography I would give it the modest title: it could be different. It cannot be otherwise. What could be different is not the bursting of the volcano or the storm grazing the coast. Cast in the midst of life's lonely shadows the difference was in selection of a theme for a flaming song. Madness imposed upon me her many forms. The madness of creation absorbed my attention when I raised my soul to the intensity of a cobra ready to strike. I was writing as if I had to strike sense into the numb bones of my fingers. I was paralyzed by unhappiness of the world. I struck as I wrote. The universe existed in one single glance of one black eye that emanated from who knows where. Were there other such eyes. I toyed with the notion of creation. It is easier to understand life if we did not have to think about creation. The living of life was in the magic of the present that made it possible to think of past and future. It was madness for sure. It could not have been otherwise. Echoes of madness I discovered in valleys where the sun took off from the sea never to return. The sea waited for the sun like mothers wait for children after dark. The sun was lost among hills. The panorama was painted with colors of pain. With men of reason I was a woman of words. I wore pain on my eyes as if they were a pair of colored spectacles and saw a different world out there. All that my eyes saw were faces of children. I could not cry because there were no tears left in the sockets of my eyes.

The rain had washed them away. With the conception that death is no more real than a banana skin I lived the day as if it were neither first nor the last. I was a singer before the song as eyes that speak before the veil give a slant to words. The song remade me in a way as the veil remakes eyes. The song of eyes opened windows to let in light through the veil of passion. Darkness met light and I remembered that I had died before I lived. Simulated passions were the only real ones. I simulated my face for stages that were dissimulated. I did not think that echoes of my song were universal. If I did not return you to yourself how would you know that I love you. The mirror has many faces and one of them happens to be me. Who are those others that I thought I knew and how well did I know them. The singer came into the world without karma. She listened to the heartthrob of muffled voices and hysterical screams that brought the stars down from the roof of the sky. That was a song without karma. Neither did life nor the world have a pattern. The pattern is external to the soul. This explains the anarchist tendencies in children and the very basis of an anarchist society that rejects sex-as-object and money as the institutional bases of life. The singer has no karma but to work and rework on existing patterns. The stars have a pattern. That is not a human pattern because it has an entirely different time frame. To stars I offer mud. The stars bow down with the grace of dancers after a grand performance. The nights are alive. I look for the souls of men and women. Their bodies respond with a tremor when the moon drowns them in her light. Such a light on a night when the body creates its own karma I am not destined to be a star nor find meaning beyond the realm of possibilities I take from science what is useful to alleviate suffering of the living world the unconditional love of people as I see them in their daily struggles is religion and the beauty of

that struggle is art that life can be bettered is the essence of
political economy but all distinctions are rendered useless
when it comes to that wonder of your face that makes
my heart sing for joy.

Footsteps

The smell of a body was enough and I was pregnant those
eyes were fresh milk I understood what footsteps meant
through waiting for another it was waiting for footsteps that
made me a poet I knew you as a person would know a
person and I knew you as a woman would know another
tears of repentance took my eyes on a ride from paradise I
fell into a desert of thorns the hills are without limits when
a child looks at them but the feet of the child are on earth
she plays without the intention of playing the way the blind
know one coin from another I could measure footsteps with
my ears the sense of precision came from birds in the rain
morality preceded religion and when language was an
instrument to understanding a situation it did not contribute
to life of the language the language degenerated into empty
clichés morality is in language that situations bring to life in
your footsteps I knew that life had a rhythm the dialectical
fusion of the artist with the actor is no facile matter
footsteps in the garden of becoming the essences of our
senses inspired by footsteps I wrote about footsteps I
endowed them with a feeling of eternity everything I lacked
turned into sound of footsteps music fused with silences
when the shapes of footsteps were characterized differently
from the sounds squeezed as lemon juice my feet barely
reached the door imagination is porcelain it breaks into tears
to the melody of june showers otherness is highest form of
oneself it hurts when I walk pregnancy affects the back this
child is harder on my body than all children that women
have ever brought into this world the footsteps never
arrived only sound at the door new silences are trajectories
of old hurts heaven was outside the door in a friendship of
ideas I searched for salvation and found the torment of

footsteps leading to imaginary encounters they were breezy times I was a woman with a sense of sunlight I tiptoed because I did not want to be heard footsteps have a way of remaining in air the breeze carried them into ears of my soul the sweetness of imagination when the other is not myself her footsteps are the blue moon on a white sky my world was clear as a quiet night when there were no footsteps figments of light on a housetop where the sun rests in the house a dream waits to be dreamt by a dreamer the nights are dizzy the waiting dream takes the form of footsteps life is a dancing bear to the staff of a gypsy fate I am not thinking of life when I think of you the footsteps of a cloud rising to the sky I slept flat on my pregnant belly I woke up in the morning ready to puke the baby must be fragile I must have squeezed her the rest of the day I had a violent headache my poor baby she affects me when her feet kick my stomach I rejoice in her footsteps as if she were the ship of days floating on waters of time she clings to my body that spoils my privacy will she grow up to steal my lovers I pity the poor thing she has nowhere to go but the pond of my belly pain is the dove passion the raven the dove is instigated to express the raven is pleasured to perform spring is season of doves passion is dance of the dead my eyes are swollen I cried because you looked into my eyes and the downpour of words did not stop I know where I stand I am not blind to who I am that which is given without any giving is love I want the gift and not the giving the waves are not obliged to moon for shining upon them I don't want words to distract me from loving you I know I am weak but I am also pregnant with memories of shadows I bring a shadow from one world of mine into another philosophy is nostalgia of the dreamer I am as unphilosophical as you can imagine I can make potatoes out of a coherent argument and sauce from a book of political

thought I can also make a child from footsteps of my lovers
give me your footsteps and my worlds are yours conditional
love is conditional not love my worlds are unconditionally
yours and the fragrance of your footsteps are mine as well
because I am yours and you choose to give
what is yours to yourself.

Interpreters and Changers

The interpreter of images and the changer of coins. I ran away from a drizzle. I met a storm along the way. I see stretch marks of my pregnancy. My skin is going soft on my leg. I put on weight in my first pregnancy. My tummy gets more and more big. The hair on my leg is growing. The celebration of mourning and arrival of a friend from a hidden galaxy of the past. I long and long to discover the elusiveness of what I long for. Coins change hands among beggars and prostitutes. The brothel and street abound in interpretations of images. Reality takes the image of a coin. It does not dissolve in a glass of salt water. A coin might be primitive. The changers of paper notes and subversions of interpretation. The marketing of art and the art of marketing. I went to buy water in the market. Unable to forgive my body dipped its head in water. I changed the currency I had in my purse. Did water cost money when the world began. On this simple principle I went out to subvert the world. The changer of words and interpreter of currencies. The engagement of literature for subversion of currencies. The inscrutable private walls of currency. Life did not begin with me but it might end with me. I swallow fate in the form of money. I talk to you about love. I ask you if you love me for who I am. Your thoughts are too long for me. My legs suffer when I start walking with your thoughts. One thought from you is all I want. Uncapturable is the poetry of change. I bought a piece of bread and all I thought was about bread. My belly refused to let me change my thoughts. Changers of the world and interpreters of living. I am not beyond myself. I am an arrow that cuts through breeze in order to reach a certain destination. The breeze does not bleed because it is a disembodied reality.

The heart bleeds that is embodied in things. I interpreted hearts as being apart from things. I changed things for things and hearts for things. The isolation of hearts and the indifference of things. Things did not change in life. I remain at one point in time. I have the vivid curiosity of a five year old and longings of a fifty five year old. My sensitivity to life is how I choose to define the woman who constituted the soul of mine. I tried to miss nothing. I missed everything. The one who tries the hardest not to miss is one who misses the most. I missed the game of exchanging open-ended interpretations with lovers. Then came definitions. No change was possible once things were defined. It was an era of systematization of definitions. I interpreted in order to change. Every other interpretation was an enclosure. Intellectual cages are redundant for swimmers of cosmic seas. Verandahs. Tropical verandahs. There are neither dwellers nor exiles over here. The street was a verandah for the child. She saw through eyes of a word. She played until play became the ethic of her body and soul. My womb is a verandah and the soul of my playing child makes me sing a song my lips cannot interpret. It rains on high seas. Water makes love to water. The sea of the horizon. In that dance of raindrops falling on sheets of silver waves I remembered sunshine, verandah and the cruelty of a man. The cruelty stayed the longest in the interiors of my body. I longed for the verandah to return into my life along with sunshine. Man's cruelty burnt my soul in the heat of open spaces. I did not want to go to heaven. I wanted to be everywhere. I never understood the cruelty of my oppressor. My own cruelty kept memory rich with wet mist of disappearing love. My interpretations were speckled with projections of a self that I thought was mine. I believe in the innocence of words that can give expression to the worst forms of cruelty. In a verandah I am a changer and an interpreter at home. Literature is married to the world. Each confirms the otherness of other. Interpretation for the sake of interpretation makes no reference to the other. Change is hallmark of a literature of innocence. Love is in painful knowledge of haunting details. The world does not fail to observe the ramifications of words. Words in the verandahs of my soul. They bask in the music of masticating mirrors.

Dust in Dreams of Beloved

Explicit intentions are not for long pregnant summers. I inhale dust in dreams of my beloved. Her body carries in her the scent of separation. I float in dust of her dreams. When I know that I'll not see her again I want to die. The separation is phenomenal and is unaffected by intentions. Pregnant I feel the longing of waves for night. From dreams of the beloved I collected a handful of dust and left for another village. I cut across a mountain path before I saw the village of my dreams. I hid behind a shadow and watched dreams go down the lanes of girlhood. Sitting on a rock I breathed the air from a field of fresh carrots. When the world is on fire I will still be craving for raw mangoes and salt with red pepper. Not so much my beloved as the dust of her dreams. Dust that does not irritate the face. Upon that dust my feet walked as if they were in a dream. This wild horse of a beloved was my early youth smiling at me. In a language I understood we made love. In a language that I did not understand love was born. I knew it was love because it was not me who made flowers fall my eyes had left my soul to find the lake of dust made from dreams of my beloved who weeps for a star that dies in an anonymous galaxy the spider of a universe quietly weaves its webs the black widow that has devoured its mate is the universe of perceptions I share in its pregnant sense of humor the moon-rose is the last rose the phase of the rose is the last of moons to come in contact with earth before the solar death on a piece of bread I inscribed the name of my beloved letters of her name added up to nothing I ate bread and nothingness of her name I fixed terms of passion my pregnant body was clumsier than usual but I was happy that my soul knew that it had no choice but to disappear with my body my soul more pregnant with the dark than with light my soul made it to moonlit markets the seller gave his body and the buyer wanted green tomatoes they spoke about exterior profiles with a sentimental value women in style are mesmerized by the essential rose of my blooming pregnancy the lunar landscape of a woman's body the woman in me came into style when I touched the forehead of the sun with a cloth and wiped the eyes of sleepy mother moon that was a language of bridges that stood on the foam of melting time I strode toward the uncanny my senses were outside my body I was elsewhere making collages the mind aged faster than body the uncanny complexes of body I am a sinister duck from watery realms the key to my heart is in a bird on the topmost branch of a tree standing on a hill in the remotest corner of earth I am a stylized woman I admit to being lost in time when I was looking for spaces I am a conglomerate of spaces unto myself I am also a seeker of grapes and the truth of grapes in wine of the beloved's dreams I saw dust on authentic mirrors that rejected faciality it is harder to forget than to remember what is remembered is sealed beyond the range of fountains of light I pursued what I could not remember in my pregnancy my body was dying to know who I was before the child came into the world I pursued fountains and whenever I saw one I became naked and gave myself to those dark waters my protruding belly was a joke to bystanders I danced the dance of waters trickling down my ticklish belly I was laughing and tears of joy ran down my face and breasts and navel and pudenda my feet moved for no reason other than move they moved to places they walked into dreams of the beloved inscrutable are the dreams like a woman's heart and the dust of madness afflicts my feet my contractions began I remembered nothing of breaking waters except one face the gentleness of one stayed through pain of skies ripping

mountains clutching the entrails of earth I cried for the face
my tears were for eyes streaming into the sanctum
sanctorum of my body I remembered what I had not
forgotten but took the shape of dusty dreams the face of my
beloved in those moments passed to return into that
prelinguistic lightning and nonverbal thunder of
my rhythmic belly.

Cloud and Ravine

Seething with discontent among shadowless objects.
Pregnancy turned me into a bundle of nerves. I felt like a
ravine with a cloud inside me. I was with my lover and I
thought of my friend. I hugged the lover's body and tears
that raged my eyes were thoughts of my friend surfacing on
the skin of my body. My lover has the delicacy of oyster
and my friend the luster of a pearl. You my friend I see a
want of love in your heart. You my lover how you wish
that I could be your friend. In my soul are two bodies. My
lover came out of smoke of a magic lamp. My friend is the
smell of cinnamon. Blinded by smoke I found my way out
of a cave guided by smell of the friend's body. The magic of
the cave took me back into the lover's arms. I missed being
lost. One body in me hungers for friendship and another
thirsts for love. I am a body divided into souls. If my body is
night I am divided as stars of cosmos. Light harps on my
skin when I remember that I am yet to be born in a moment
that has not yet arrived. The cloud in me grew bigger and
the ravine of my body opened its arms to receive the cloud.
The arms embraced the cloud without enclosing. I was
breathing clouds of fire until the dew of my friend's lips
calmed my flaming eyes. I love you because you are
nothing. I want to be loved because I am nothing. Ravenous
clouds among cloudy ravines. My body is immaterial. My
love disappoints me and my friendship disguises the
disappointment. Why is my soul quiet as a street with no
people on it. Bitter truths burn the tongue. My heart is a
bystander. The rain that touches the ground loses its
visibility in depths of the soil and has the character of
history caught in a dream without knowing what the dream
is about. Hurt is otherness of death. History is the condition

of hurt. The rain is not aware that it is part of history. The hurt shares in the indifference of rain. Invisible hurts of an invisible history. I see nothing and I am obsessed by what I do not see. The passages that lead from today to yesterday. There was no tomorrow. The sun did not rise the day after.

It stopped with yesterday. What are shadows without hurts. They would disappear into utter emptiness. Why do shadows struggle to stay as shadows. The shadows whose destiny is forgotten and destroyed by the dark. I hate light. That shallow bringer of memories. Roused by reflections the shadows mimic themselves. You were the real sleeping on my breasts. The one growing inside my womb. When I thought of you there were no shadows because there was no sky above me. I was outside the universe. My soul experienced a sense of familiarity that had nothing to do with days or nights. The pregnant universe and its shapeless body. I smiled wondering if I projected my body upon the states of the universe. My shapeless feelings and the critical body of my friend. The warmth of my glance and the picture of my lover. The fragile equation of lover and friend that bends to nothing. I don't see you and the curse of days is upon me. My lover who is my friend. My friend who keeps me in a state of love. My tongue stands for longing, language and kissing. Orange, moon and roses are my favorite symbols. Art, death and semiotics are discourses that my imagination is glad to delve. The making of a voice is yearning of the cloud for the ravine. The production of life happens twice in the same moment. Once as light flowing from a fountain in paradise and once as the ghost of a rose outside the window of a lover. Echoes of voices of shadows fill the air of night. The shadows of echoes of voices return as memories. Transitions transcend the cloud and ravine. You thief of thieves. My friend and lover. I forsook worlds for you. You gave me the image of your

eyes looking in my direction. You might have been
watching a cloud carefully descend into depths
of a yawning ravine.

Recurring Kaleidoscopes

Changing times are recurring kaleidoscopes. I met you before you came into this world. I came from you. Because of you I am myself. I was you before I took the avatar of myself. I am a version of you. Is my child a version of me or am I a version of her. I cannot ask you the same question because you are not my mother and I am not your child. You do not avail yourself through a concept. You are my lover at times, my child and my mother. I change my versions as you change yours. Pregnant I was angry at the world. With all the malice that I could muster I hated this thing called life. I wanted to murder for the joy of murdering. I could decimate the skies in a matter of seconds and stamp the hearts of men flat out of existence. I was everywhere in pregnancy. My face in the mirror looked beautiful for some inexplicable reason. My body insisted on changing lovers just to feel the need for change. I cannot be with a person whose heart is not with me. I took her heart before I took her into myself. In my pregnancy I recurred for the sake of recurrence. The intolerable pressure of work made me look for excitement. The excitement was no more real than the work itself. Time does not pass and I cry that my tears will melt the heart of time into moving like a magician's wand and drift me away from nostalgic journeys of killing ordinariness. The passing of wind brings no messages. The towel in the bathroom has more to give. The room was without windows and the night showed no sign of the coming of day. Either I had to meet you or die. I died before I met you. My sense of privacy I gave nobody. My body was the world you knew. It was invisible. I interpreted your feelings to it. My body was calm as sea after sunset. She was alone. My body knew what she was never taught.

The knowledge recurred like wild patterns of a kaleidoscope. The wickedness of a non-existent time came out as pangs of desire. Those pangs dominated my disintegrated spirit for the time that I waited for thorns on a briar to change to immaculate roses. Love was in a miraculous elegance connected to windows without vistas. A world without time had its non-recurring patterns. That was a proof of pencils having preceded pendulums. Life and its objects. The pencils wrote about life before pendulums reminded us of objects. I sprang out of the egg of a meaningless idiom called language. The egg was there before the chicken never to recur. The grandfather was before the father. The grandmother was never not there. I am passionate but never sexual. The wild imagination came like a bolt from blue. Impassioned by a kaleidoscope in the sky I committed myself to a series of memoirs of a small world in the forgotten sea of unknowing. It seems as if life had begun a moment ago and never left that moment. I bear the child of the feminine person. I stare back at eyes that take me away from the kaleidoscope of my nature. In all first meetings goodbyes are implicit. In my pregnancy I borrowed the one from you and became the other. I am not certain if I will miss you. I have a child to think about. This child is a recurrence of my childhood. I was a girl who felt the hooves of horses in her veins. My mother kept me alert through the middle of night with her tales of djinns. She never failed to fall asleep watching my curious eyes. The pregnancy made me busy up to my throat. My face is free to discover your sensuality. I never sensed you before. You were in other patterns of light. You loved me and I followed you like a star to ends of earth. In the light of the star you levitated and came into my breast. My eyes brought the child in you out in the open. You stood fearful on an empty road afraid of what was to come. A song was playing as you looked at a flock of cranes flying high in the sky. Death stood next to you ready to take you in its arms. I turned death into a child and hid her in my womb. A brief element in my body died before death assumed the form of life in my womb. You recurred as chaos in the kaleidoscope of my being.

Lips of Sun

Bewildered by loss of senses I resorted to lips of sun. My
lusty encounters did not cease with pregnancy. I squeezed
the sun between lips. I was not in my senses. I was in a
container of salt. I was salt before saltiness came into
existence. Before I knew heat or light I was the fiery lips of
sun. I chose the way of uncontainable madness. It was a
long nervous adolescence. I might have died of shame. I
lived with a sense of pity. Lost things counted for points in
my heart. You traveled between various points within
borderless skylines of my heart. The pleasure was mine in
the shade of sunny lips. Wet with excitement my lips
resurrect images of butterflies. Time is appendage to the
timeless. Timeless are spaces of bodies in which I make and
unmake bread of all shapes and sizes. The bread of love is
not meant for consumption. Baked by lips of the sun the
bread of love is for the benevolent. My benevolence is
limited to grass. I ask for nothing more. Out of pity I took
joy in the joys of others. Cheeks and chin and forehead and
lips I kissed the sun everywhere. The concept of house was
not made for love. The sun of love is without a conception.
The owners of the moment are slaves of faces without time.
Even when the technology of words becomes empty and
the sentence in mind is built without a material base I
understand your longings. They are longings of one who
has denied matter. I let those longings rub the surfaces of
skin. Technologized words. Words emulate other words.
Other words are words with no other in them. I never asked
for no words. Meaning stood for otherness of words. They
were only more words. The bed of flowers was watered
with words from a can of meanings. Your eyes are traitors
to your lips. They speak the inexpressible but your lips lie.

If I were one of your lips I would be careful not to let a message slip into the kingdom of eyes. They are agents of the enemy in camaraderie with my other senses. The lips are at the center of brain. They know much but speak little. Turn those eyes into pearls and throw them back into mouths of oysters. Words spurn me to the extent that I do not spurn them. I envy those time periods in history where the woman stood on a low rock and memorized lines written on sand. Time did not need to stand in the frame of reference of the timeless. The rock was a particle of sand that had grown into rock. That took away from the rock the pretense of infallibility. On those fallible rocks of desire I discovered that words were sand that came out of lips of the sun. History is a prison that only one in prison can uncover. The present is a shadow over the past. You neither let me be nor let me go. I want the clothes of the person to change and not the person. The person is a prelude to song. How could the song exist without the prelude or clothes without the person. Changing clothes are for passing days. The person is for lips of the sun. Nothing was written before nothing came into existence as a discourse of nothingness. The sun emerged from lips of a woman. Mindless was the sun but those lips were waves of fire that ran in every possible direction. If not heat it was the mosquitoes. We made love as a matter of fact. You locked yourself to my pregnant body. For a minute I wondered if you were not the child to come. The heat brought mosquitoes with it and the mosquitoes did not allow us to sleep until past midnight. Love occupied our brains. The fire of eyes made us forget sleep. The lips of the sun did not move. I was the mother I was denied and the father I never had. I am the child I always was. The child in me is pregnant with a child. Quiet were those lips like the sweet mouth of a sleeping child. I moved my lips toward lips of the sun. They quivered as if touched by a dream at night.

Cumin and Mustard

Cumin does not blend with mustard. It retains its heavenly
flavor. Mustard does not sacrifice its bitterness in exchange
for flavor of cumin. The bitterness of my intelligence does
not blend with the flavor of your body. Blending is a state of
mediocrity. I refuse to blend. Blending was never my style.
I did not blend with the unborn inside me. She is an
offshoot of my imagination. She is inside me and lives
outside me. Memory is made of moments while life is made
of days and nights. My moments are dead in prison. I blend
to the point where I am not you. I am just myself and my
intelligence rots away. I can't taste the flavor of your body.
When you spent time with me there was this nervous edge
to it. Cumin is for body and mustard for soul. The soul of
mustard you are and the body of cumin I am. In warm oil
cumin becomes cumin by virtue of its smell while the palate
releases the bitterness of mustard. Disappeared but not
forgotten. I appeared in moments that triggered memory.
It was not coincidence. I was called and I obeyed in the
humility of a dancer moving her feet to the rhythm of
music. Music was master and my body a slave. Not of
music but love. Music was the intermediary between love
and body. The lover sees clearly at night. The woman of
taste is the mother of the child. I waited for the lover
when the woman of taste was away. Mustard was my
lover and the woman of taste was cumin. My lover was
destiny and the woman of taste was my fate. My destiny
was not to be seen in the day. My fate stuck to me like glue.
Destiny was chance I created inside me. My fate was given.
At some point my destiny turned into fate. Fate never left
destiny alone. In those moments I called fate the serpent. I
moved in destiny while I waited in fate. In mirrors I look

for destiny to break the chains of fate. I turned my destiny into an escape artist. My fate outsmarted me with preparedness of a defense lawyer who anticipated the story of the witness. I wrote stories only to prove that I had a destiny. I slept on the concept of feelings. The hand that felt the earth had green fingers. The lover dispenses with time and energy and hope. The child in me is image of the lover. The child belongs to the woman of taste. The child was fated to be born as I'm fated to smile in spite of pain. I visualized her face as if it were my own. In my destiny I saw her become a woman. God the absent lover comes in my dreams in the shape of a mustard seed. I took God between my teeth and savored it with my tongue. The woman of taste had a thing for cumin. When she spoke of what I meant to her I smelt cumin in her mouth. I understood her sincerity. My fate cannot accept the fact that I've a destiny. The cruelty of necessity I countered with mountains of cumin and seas of mustard. Feelings are ironic blenders of tastes and smells. The lethargy of uncoded expectations clusters of them arrive in droves seducing the sleeper the mattresses that come and become who I am moments are multiplied in the momentum of birds that take off into wilderness of fantasy in work my love derived the singularity of cumin that looked for burning mustard I made a choice between the solver of mysteries and the daunting mystery of aromatic bodies with fingers on their foreheads I chose the mystery in the soul of the solver of mysteries the imagination of a person was a womb that could be touched by the fingers of a woman the pregnant imagination that soldered the wine of the lover's breath with the meekness of the woman of taste in pungent odors I discovered that the symbolic value of love cannot be at variance with the material value intrinsic to discourses the lover in the woman of taste and the taste of love in the

hands of the wine maker for the wine of a body I rebelled
against the bitterness of age in pregnancy I cultivated the
wisdom of inserting music into poetry destiny is intuition in
response to a mindless fate I intuited that cumin tinged with
mustard is the message of my nonplussed eyes leaping
across rivers of bodies in heat into that white tent where
your naked self quietly lies under a
rubble of thoughts.

Moral Prisms

Deprived I was depraved. My cheeks suffered the pain of giving. Depths took on a character denied to heights. I reached depths of depravity during heights of deprivation. The heights were false as tips of nails. In pregnancy my nails grew longer than usual. Only the tips were false. I did not love my nails less. Not even in deprivation. My depravity made me appreciate the rest of my nails apart from the tips. Music, moonlight and the unborn nucleus of a rose in my belly. Loving men and resisting women. Either I die or this system. Will you be mother to my child if she does not fit into the category of normal. Your suffering is mine but do not leave the child by herself. I fear the loss of the child and the arrival of long days condemned to quietness of prisons. I want to live and measure the length of time that life may open the doors of sweetness. Is my heart darker than night sky. Tears revolved around sockets of the eye. They refused to come out. The waters of places I had drunk from brought me back to those places. You perceived me in parts that were not my whole. Your visions of my wholeness missed the line of my neck that could hold a string of pearls. What was I that you could never know. I waited for mornings when I did not have to wait anymore. In proclaiming I am one with you I declare my difference from all. I speak and my words are cubes of salt washed back into the sea. I think and my thoughts are silent spectators to workings in my soul. I dream and there is no time to make it real. Passing times are stray dogs inevitable as sand that borders seas. Morality is prism of light. Through moral prisms I gave a touch of humility to light. Did the prism share with light a common ancestry in the night of shared feelings. Morality was in petals on which teardrops fall with slow motion of windows opening to notes of a flute. I was pregnant with the night. Was my child the dawn of untimely hopes. Penultimate to all hopes is consciousness of life as essence of matter. Matter is self-perpetuating mother of life. Morality is acknowledgment of material world through prisms of the senses. I am indefinable nothing that barely lends herself to interpretation. I did not appropriate the world. I merely sensed it. I could sense you without appropriation. I am a prism that alters meanderings of light. I was senseless at dusk when the world came into being. I could not have known it unless I stayed in your body to figure out the configuration of planets and their relation to stars. It was anarchy that kept me going. I was not searching for a soul. A shapeless body came toward me in shape of my self. It had the shape of a word that was unsaid that was heard but could not be memorized the word that did not point toward silence and did not play with the idea of nothing the word that led to every other word was in the tapping of your fingers on a keyboard I was floating in fear I woke up to a noise in a deafeningly quiet forest I moved into mountains before I entered plains I was a woman of villages I relished my past in the forests I espoused the communism of differences the raindrop that fell into sea contributed to the character of the sea from which it emerged to the sea of light I give the darkness of my womanhood I had to change the world before I could love it I learnt to love the reality of change I accepted life through the gift of consciousness there were no givers because I was what I had received the gift of nothing unknowing myself was the only way I could know you the giver of gifts the word that meant nothing it was a moral position that I imbibed through prisms of discourses I cultivated the prismatic knowledge of the lover of eyes I had to know the ground before I could write I was insecure of certain grounds where my heart raged and my hand stood still I moved for the sake of words I changed the grounds on which I stood for that one word that brought peace I gave up thinking of dying sunsets with no more dawns to arrive.

Purity of Sound

In time I was a woman of space. The birth of a child is a
spatial process that begins with the body and ends in soul.
My love of a woman who endows my spatiality with reason
is out of the bounds of temporal. I am a woman among
women who are conscious of their personas. My name is
written on pillars of blue reflections that stand upon clouds.
To live history is not the same as to write about it. I sleep
for the love of waking. Awake I seek the purity of sound
where words arrive at a consensus with music and silence.
The sound of nothing is pure because there is no sound.
The raindrop rushes back into the cloud. The tree returns to
seed. The pregnant woman is a child in her mother's womb.
My word is the idea of sound in hands that performed in the
dark. I broke through rays of stubborn sunlight with the
beams of night. Life poses questions that life does not
answer. I found the answer in a flower in a woman's hair.
Love is meaningless as cruelty when nature seems pitiless as
man I see cold grisly rain and a human being at the bus stop
asleep wound in a gunny bag colder eyes stay away from
the sight the poor that neither wake in their beds nor return
home to sleep a blankness has set in the hearts of hawkers
who work day in and out with no hope of making things
any better they anticipate nothing and nothing happens the
question of the past of the world is as unimportant as the
future a person's voice is distinct while the rest of body
decays the process of decay produces the distinctness the
voice places unceasing demands upon life establishing the
purity of sound the warbling of waves without origins and
nowhere to go the only reality that a dream can aspire to is
knowledge of dreaminess a friend like a star is born out of
sweet nothingness does the drop need the ocean for it to

exist as a drop I cannot die except by chance I choose a friend for life my friend the bearer of tears that look like my own I bore you in my veins music and death were themes that dominated my youth music disturbed the patterns of my day at night my tortured head wanted to die neither music nor death but you my friend the materiality of the voice the groaning of the mother and cry of the new-born the spirit of sound the purity of silence unknown to ears the morning you left the form of my body changed from light blue to purple I knew that you were momentary but the memory of you was a prison without a skylight I was a child who could not know her sadness there were no tears on my face only a smile that formed a thin layer of snow on my bleeding heart I saw you in my soul's mirror you were there the ocean that did not require the drop for it to be the ocean if fate is a sleeping lion that dare not be tempted I put my finger in the mouth of that lion to see if the color of my blood has changed in the absence of a ghost that I loved those transparent feelings that one sees in faces of actors who try to be themselves as actors in the characters they portray I bared my swollen belly to the winds will my child come to light knowing separation I live in the light of separation I bear a child inside me who does not know time my belly has the shape of a raw mango I pass a kiss from lips of my lover to my belly the sea makes me sick I throw out I am filled with heaviness and nausea you come back into mind I replicated the meaning of light in separation from you bathed in milk of ages I shot the raindrop with a gaze I practiced the histrionics of voice with purity of a hiss from a serpent guarding the doors of a castle I wept as I sang hearing my own voice the pulse of my being stopping at odd intervals the requiem of lost love the tenor of time in a closed room the life I lead was a process of dying each moment I died waiting for the next I optimized on reality I spiced it with illusion in order to make it palatable the bitter had to be sugared that's how places entered memory or else places would be places and memory would be a container with a hole at the bottom the purity of sound was in irretrievable quietness of a dancer's belly snaking into depths of the earth.

Elusive Runner

Caravanserai but where are the caravans. I ran with the imagination that there was a destiny that anticipated my coming. It seemed I was alone at all times. I had spells of dizziness. My stomach protested at slightest stress. My body could not accept changes in weather with grace. I never worked a day for a life. As a girl I used the word madness interchangeably with sanity. That's how I saw the constructedness of bourgeois life. I lust for sweetness of life but I was in love with death. I moved between naked worlds. Clothes made no difference for one who spent evenings dancing for no reason to eyes of strangers in a caravanserai. They were no strangers but eyes that had the strange look that happens to eyes waking in middle of a dream of time waking from an instant of nothing. The actress does not die possessive as she is about a face that loves nothing more than to wake up dead. In the thought of giving up this nervous body I became the girl with the voice of a woman rising as daylight from the tranquility of dawn. I knew my body just as well as my body knew me. They were solitary instants when I knew the body of otherness. I saved myself from demons of sanitation when I embraced the dirt of the world. I bought my freedom subjugating my soul to imaginations of the body. My soul quivered at the sight of caravans in a distance. My body fed the eyes of my thirsty soul with mirages. My soul cried for waters of perfection. My soul was an elusive runner and my body was the amanuensis to a concatenation of signs. History is the poetry of transition. The lover's body that speaks through misread gestures. The voice that does the misreading. The eyes that conspire against that voice. The caravans that my eyes created my voice dispelled as winds dispel the dust of reason in the lover's soul. I see emptiness of morning at nights in the arms of lovers. I change lovers as they change me that each morning must look different from the previous one. I could not bear the thought that the universe was composed of just one morning that endlessly reproduced itself at the end of nights without end. Out of vestiges of passing nights I reproduced the bodies of lovers endlessly. I bore my children in the fecundity of deserts. Lunar sands strike my heaving body. Alone I wander through a caravanserai. Naked I am among the clothed. I see the clothes. The person is an extension of my loneliness. There is no other but the otherness of what looks like myself. I die that the life of my fingers may reach out to vacant bodies that hold me through successive ages. There is no death for the lover that waits for me with eyes of the dying. She dies and is born through me. I live in her as a moment. That moment is an unvisited mansion meant for the poor of this world. I make my moments as I move through mansions dreaming of arriving caravans. I run to elude a thing called myself that follows the shadow of the other. I run for life on streets of death. I recall names of my love as if that were my calling. I transgress to give desire a semblance of meaning. I am born through that act of transgression. I am my own mother. In the womb of timeless fantasies I make myself as picture of the real. My language is clearer than my thoughts unless I let words betray secrets of my searching soul to unrelenting body. My heart wrestled with the heart within it. My blood turned hot while tears rained down the face of my soul. I soiled my clothes running through muddy roads. In your dream I was a silkworm. I spun stories as if they were cocoons. A silken night was your dream. We moved through impressionistic hallways with filaments of red warming the air and curtains of dew cooling the light. Desire I combined with a sacred sense of laughter. I desired to reveal what was elusive in nature. The world was at my doorstep. I desired to change it with the knowledge that it was changeable. I ran naked and alone. I left emptiness behind that some wandering cloud might take pity upon.

Pearls of an Unstrung Necklace

I am a pearl on the neck of the queen of Sheba. I am the
queen worshipping the sun in the long arms of Solomon.
I'm Solomon in the womb of Bathsheba. I am naked
Bathsheba in the eyes of David bathed in rivers of lust. I am
Nathan the prophet who gave language to justice of God. I
am Uriah the innocent whose blood bore knowledge of
coming death so unlike a lamb that cannot conceive
meaning of death by betrayal. I reckon I must be different if
I trace my lineage to a black pearl touched by a hand that
unstrung the necklace as if it were a knot that prefigured the
workings of the soul. Ethiopia at the feet of the queen and
the lips of Solomon sealed on her belly. The past is an
empty shell and I feel no love for open windows that broke
my heart as a child. When King Lear speaks of nothing
coming out of nothing he refers to floating clouds on
fictitious skies. Gautama the Buddha's nothingness is the
child coming out of womb. Shakespeare is a humanist and
Gautama a revolutionary. Humanism disconnects itself
from its situatedness. If forms are empty then the signature
of the Buddha is a joke and language the paradox that
accommodates the situatedness of things. In the films of
Mizoguchi women are not innocent in the classical sense of
the term. Their martyrdom is calculated to touch the
conscience of a patriarchy that has none. They subsist on
the notion that death is preferable to life without the hope
of dignity. Uriah's innocence aims to transform and
humanize the patriarchal David. In the process Uriah loses
his manhood and turns into a trusting child. Bathsheba lives
that history may be inscribed on her body. She makes
history stand on its feet when she chooses to enter the bed
of David and feign complete ignorance of the murder of her

working class husband. Lying on the royal bed of Israel Bathsheba recollects the smell of Uriah's body. One form of betrayal is avenged through another. She is pregnant with Uriah's firstborn Solomon. The conception took place through a concept. Thought became word and the word passed into nothing. The shadow of a river and ripples from the disappearance of shadows under the canopy of a catkin cathected with the enervating rage of lust in the dreamer's body. The innocent live in terror of innocence. Wild with demands of lust imposed by an erotic imagination the sequence of moments are sequestrated to form cubicles of isolation. David was in fact the tiger and Uriah the lamb. The pearl on the neck of the queen of Sheba is no more innocent than Bathsheba searching for truth of her husband's death in David's eyes. I give my love to phenomenally clear absent bodies. The truth of innocence is where the lamb in tiger is also tiger in the lamb. Unstrung pearls are the beginning of the secret wisdom of Buddha.

The truth of the pearl is in knowledge of sea before the hand of time brought land out of the sea as a separate entity. Land that is no more innocent than a child. I am the sea the home of the pearl. I am innocent as the body of the Buddha that thrives on imminence of change. I bring out truths concealed in processes of humanizing truth. I have a pearl of a heart when it comes to necks of queens. I am Uriah who laughs at the fatuousness of a king. I am Bathsheba who subverts patriarchy from the center of its being. I live as black light of a pearl. I am the pearl that disturbs the evenness of beds of kings. Before destiny comes the Buddha's smile. The smile that anticipates destiny like the mother the child. I am the smile of Buddha before she went to her last sleep. The smile that was a pearl and I had not yet died. We saw ecstatic days in open fields and our voices synchronized with wind in the mountains the moment was

in the neck of a queen Sheba the mother of Israel her son-
lover the child in me looked at water snakes moving
importunately like lines of sand in a desert from one end of
a dream to another my articulation took the form of an
amnesiac reviving fantasies of the real the eyes of rain
sparkle like pearls of an unstrung necklace and
sweetness overtook our longings with
the innocence of running waters
at the crest of
darkness.